Addie: To Wager on Her Future

Addie: To Wager on Her Future

Mansfield Park Continuation, Episode 5

LEENIE BROWN

LEENIE B BOOKS
HALIFAX

Cover design by Leenie B Books. Images sourced from Deposit Photos and Period Images.

ISBN (print) 978-1-989410-36-3; (ebook) 978-1-989410-35-6

Contents

Dear Reader,

At the end of *Mansfield Park*, Jane Austen wrote:

> Let other pens dwell on guilt and misery. I quit such
> odious subjects as soon as I can, impatient to restore
> everybody not greatly in fault themselves to tolera-
> ble comfort and to have done with all the rest.

It is my goal in writing the books found in the *Other Pens,
Mansfield Park Series* to take up my pen and dwell, in part,
on those Austen characters who were at fault in some way
in *Mansfield Park*.

These stories do not comprise a retelling or even a vari-
ation of Miss Austen's work. They begin after the close
of *Manfield Park* with Henry Crawford deciding to prove
himself worthy of a good woman. From there, the ripples
of change spread out to influence the lives of others in his
circle of family and friends, encompassing a wide cast of
original characters, as well as some from *Mansfield Park*.

While each episode contains a complete happily ever
after for its hero and heroine, it is assumed that the reader

knows about the events in the preceding books. Therefore, while reading in any order may be done, for maximum enjoyment, reading all of the books in order is recommended.

Chapter 1

A sheep bleated as clouds floated overhead. The sun was warm and the smell of dew dampened grass still clung to the edges of the breeze. However, all the perfectness of this spring morning was lost on Adela Atwood. Her focus was where it nearly always was — on a horse. This particular horse was a newcomer to the area and, even from a distance, he was a beauty.

"Look. See how he rises from his seat just before his horse begins to fly down the course?" Addie only spared a glance for her companion. She would not be distracted from watching such a fine beast and rider. How she wished she was still allowed to ride astride instead of constrained by society to ride aside. It was not that one could not cover a great deal of ground in a short amount of time while seated like a proper lady. It was just that one could not stand in her stirrups and urge her horse to thunder across the ground as the horse she was watching did.

"That." She spared her friend a second glance. "That is what James needs to do. He rises but not so high. Nor does he lean so far forward. Silverthorne's horses are fine animals, but they do not show as well as they could. If one – just one — of our horses could place near the front of the field — first or second, we could charge much more for the stallion's services."

It was perhaps not the sort of thing with which her aunt Edith would say a proper lady should concern herself, but her father would not reprimand her. Whenever her aunt visited, she was forever scolding Addie's father that Addie was given far too much freedom and would never make a good match if she continued as she was. Her father would always give his sister a look which said she was speaking out of turn and reply that he wagered she was wrong.

"But your brother will not listen to you," Susan Price reminded her, "for, to him, you know nothing of horses."

Addie groaned. "He has become such a ninny."

James had not always been a ninny. At one point, he had been a great friend and companion. It was his stupid friends who were the problem. They seemed to think it a great sport to make fun of her and her friends, and her brother was too complacent to not follow their lead. Why must going away to school change a fellow so much? He never used to think of her as incapable of thinking as well as he did.

"I likely know as much as he does," Addie grumbled. "It is not he who has been helping the grooms with the stables. That has been me, and do you know why? It is because he has been too busy doing whatever it is that his friends decide he should do." How she wished he would be his own man instead of following others.

"He has only this term, and then, he shall be done with school," Susan reminded her. "Surely, being away from his friends for long stretches of time will help. Will it not?"

Susan, who was as sweet as a fresh-baked apple pie, was always attempting to find the good in a situation. Unfortunately, Addie was not certain there was a great deal of good left in her older brother. If there was, it was well-hidden. The thought made her heart ache, for she missed the old James!

"Do you not think so?" Susan repeated her question.

Addie shrugged. She hoped it, but she was too uncertain to answer with a resounding yes.

"Two of his friends are set to travel once they complete their schooling." That was a good thing. "James was going to go with them until... well..." And his not going with his friends would be an even better thing except for the fact that it came at the expense of her father's condition.

Susan reached across from the grey mare on which she sat to grasp Addie's hand. "It is a terrible thing to have a father or an uncle fall ill."

And never recover, Addie added to herself. Susan still expected her uncle to regain his health and strength, but again, Addie was too uncertain to agree with her friend. Of course, a severe injury like Sir Thomas had sustained was not the same as a stroke, but the result was often the same as the patient was either left in a weakened, nearly useless condition such as her father was, or, more mercifully, succumbed to death before he was confined to his chambers to waste away during his remaining months or years. It went without saying that she would never wish death upon her friend's uncle, but, just as surely, she also could not hope for him to survive in such a state as her father did.

"I almost wish James would be gone longer than this term. Mr. Shepherd heeds my advice because it is so similar to Father's. I fear things will not go so well once James returns." They never used to argue as much as they did now. Again, she blamed his friends.

"Tom can help him," Susan offered, "and if not Tom, then Edmund. Edmund is very good with numbers and exceptionally wise."

Addie chuckled. It was just like Susan to offer help. She was excessively charitable, much like her sister Fanny. Providence had most certainly smiled upon Addie to give her friends such as Susan Price and Fanny Bertram, for Addie was given to seeing dark clouds of trouble on the horizon rather than the sunshine Susan seemed to carry around with her.

It had not always been so. Addie used to be nearly as cheerful as Susan, but then, James had gone to school (and become a ninny), her father had had two strokes in as many years, and with the last apoplectic seizure six months ago, the running of the estate had fallen largely on her for her father could no longer write or do much for himself. She could have sent for James to come home, but her father would hear nothing of keeping Jame from completing his education.

"I am certain James would benefit greatly from their assistance," Addie said. "But that is only if my brother will seek help from them."

That was likely her greatest fear in the whole ordeal. Her brother might take advice from others to help him settle into his new role as master of Silverthorne Court, but would he accept it from a knowledgeable source or would one of his friends move in and become co-master? She shuddered. If any of his friends were to do such a thing it would likely be Mr. Willet. That gentleman was as slippery as a snake and likely just as dangerous – at least, to a lady's virtue, for the gentleman was the overly friendly sort of fellow who said what he must to charm whom he willed.

She would likely find out in two week's time when the term ended.

"Have you had a good ride?" Edmund Bertram's question interrupted Addie's contemplation of her brother.

"Indeed, we have. Have we not, Addie?" Susan responded brightly. "What brings you out on this fine morning? Is Fanny well?"

Edmund chuckled. "Fanny was in perfect health when I

left the parsonage. I was looking for Tom. He had wished to discuss some particulars about the work to be done on the damaged wing of the house, but he desired to ride out with Miss Eldridge first. Have you seen them?"

Both Addie and Susan assured him that they had not and then agreed to join him on his ride for neither of them had had their fill of riding. Was it even possible for Addie to have her fill of riding?

"Have you let your mare run?" Edmund asked Susan.

"Not yet. We have been very sedately ladylike," she replied in a teasing tone.

"Indeed? I find that a trifle hard to believe since you are with Miss Atwood." Edmund's smile was warm and welcoming.

"I assure you that it is true," Addie said with a laugh.

"Then, you would not be opposed to a race to that tree on the knoll?" Edmund looked between Susan and Addie for their response.

It was not the first time that Addie had raced with Susan and her cousin. Both Susan and Edmund knew how to be all that was proper when in company, but they were not always so. There was a small longing for adventure – safe, well-regulated adventure – in both of them.

"I would find a good gallop to be most delightful," Addie assured him. Her longing for adventure was slightly greater and less well-regulated than that of her friends. She often dared to do things where they held back.

"As would I," Susan agreed. Of course, Susan's gallop would be less aggressive than Addie's. Susan was not so compelled to win races as Addie was.

"Then, move ahead of me," Edmund instructed as he always did.

Ever the gentleman, he always insisted on allowing the ladies to have a one-length advantage, and Addie seriously doubted if he ever truly gave his horse his head when racing with them. To Addie's way of thinking the advantage was unnecessary. However, Mr. Edmund Bertram was a sweet man, always looking to the needs of others whenever he saw them, or when his wife pointed them out. Therefore, she did not protest his directive even if it did make the race somewhat unfair.

Having taken her place in front of Edmund and across from Susan, Addie leaned forward and whispered a word of encouragement to her mount, a beautiful chestnut Arabian named Damon, and then, when Edmund shouted, she and her gelding were off. She continued to lean forward, urging Damon to fly.

"You always win," Susan complained with a laugh as she came to a stop a distance beyond the specified tree and next to Addie.

"Silverthorne's horses are excellent," Edmund reminded Susan.

"That they are," Addie agreed.

"And Addie is the best rider I know – who is not male, that is," Susan added.

"You know very few other female riders," Addie cautioned, although she knew herself to be a very adept horsewoman. She had not lost her seat since she was twelve. Once had been enough. Thankfully, she had not suffered any serious injury.

"I would have to agree with Miss Price."

Addie turned to see the rider she had been watching earlier. When had he approached? She did not remember seeing him anywhere near where they were.

"You ride very well," the stranger said. Then, he leaned forward and added, "Likely better than my sister, but do not tell her I said so." He winked, causing Addie to smile.

Whoever he was, he seemed a friendly sort of fellow.

"Miss Atwood," Edmund said, "I do not believe you have had the opportunity to meet Mr. Eldridge."

"No, indeed, I have not." She would have remembered meeting him.

"Miss Atwood, this is Mr. Robert Eldridge, his sister, Miss Eldridge is betrothed to Tom. Mr. Eldridge –"

Mr. Eldridge cleared his throat, and Edmund corrected himself. "My apologies, Robert, this is Miss Adela Atwood. Her father owns Silverthorne Court which borders Mansfield to the south."

The eyebrow over Mr. Eldridge's left eye arched. "Silverthorne Court?" There was a marked note of respect in the surprised question.

"I thought you would know it." Edmund chuckled. "Mr. Eldridge is also in the business of producing fine equines."

How very interesting! A handsome gentleman who knew horses at least as well as she did. Was there anything better?

"I was admiring his horse earlier. At least, I assume it was he who was riding here," Addie said to Edmund before turning to Mr. Eldridge. "Your horse runs very well."

"Hugo is the best." Mr. Eldridge gave his horse's neck a pat.

Addie's lips tipped into a smirk. "That has yet to be proven."

Both Mr. Eldridge and Edmund laughed.

"Addie is rather prejudiced," Edmund said.

"As am I." Mr. Eldridge's head tipped as he studied Damon. "There is one way we could determine the answer. We could have a short race."

"An unfair one!" Addie protested before she could think better of it.

"What do you mean?" Susan asked. "Mr. Eldridge would not cheat, would you?"

"No, I never do. I do not need to. As I said, Hugo is the best."

"Oh, goodness!"

A pretty blonde, whom Addie assumed was Miss Eldridge since she was accompanied by Tom, had approached and had heard the last comment.

"Who is my brother attempting to goad into racing?" She leveled a severe look at Mr. Eldridge.

"I am goading no one. Miss Atwood wishes for me to prove that Hugo is the best. Therefore, I suggested a short race as a way of determining the veracity of my claim."

"And I am happy to race," Addie said, "as long as the race is fair."

Mr. Eldridge scowled. "Why would it not be fair?"

"I cannot stand in my stirrups as you can," Addie answered. "Such a shift in position would give your horse an advantage that I am not afforded to give to my horse."

Tom Bertram chuckled. "She has you there."

Reluctantly, Mr. Eldridge conceded the point. "Then, I will not rise from my saddle. I am certain Hugo can still outrun –" He waved at her horse.

"Damon," she supplied.

"I am certain Hugo can still outrun Damon." He tipped his head and studied Addie's horse once more. "Or mostly certain," he added with a grin. He shook his head. "He is a fine-looking creature."

"He thanks you for the compliment. Now, where shall I prove you wrong?"

Miss Eldridge laughed. "I think I shall like you."

"Oh, Faith," Tom said, "I have been remiss in my duties.

This is our neighbour, Miss Adela Atwood. Her father's estate, Silverthorne Court, borders Mansfield to the south."

"Silverthorne?" she looked at her brother. "Is that the one you have mentioned several times as having excellent horse stock?"

Her brother nodded. "The very one."

"Addie," Tom interrupted, "this is my betrothed, Miss Faith Eldridge, though I suspect you have already deciphered that."

"It is a pleasure to meet you, Miss Eldridge," Addie replied.

"The pleasure is all mine, especially if you beat my brother."

To Addie, the relationship between brother and sister seemed to be somewhat argumentative but in a playful sort of fashion. Once again, Addie longed to have her brother back as he had been before attending school.

"From here to the fence." Mr. Eldridge pointed to their right.

"How high is the fence?"

"About three feet, I suppose. Why?" Mr. Eldridge answered.

"And is the ground clear on the other side?"

"You are going to jump it?"

Addie shrugged. "Only if necessary. Is it clear?"

"Yes," Tom answered. "I have taken it many times. It is

not a hard jump." His expression grew serious. "But do be careful. Your father does not need you injured or worse."

Tom Bertram had sustained a nasty injury in a fall when attempting to take a jump, so his concern was not founded in senseless worry. Therefore, Addie listened to it more than she would have had such a sentiment come from anyone else in their current party.

"I ask only as a precaution," she assured him.

"She'll run full out to the end," Tom said to Mr. Eldridge. "Do not push her too far."

"I wish for a fair race," Addie protested. "I will not have him treating me as a delicate flower."

Tom inclined his head. "Very well, but I know Eldridge. He'll not give an inch either. Indeed, he'll be quite blind to anything around him."

"Which is as it should be." Addie lifted her chin and smiled as if her heart was not beating faster than Damon's feet when in a full gallop. Perhaps she had challenged the wrong fellow. She leaned forward and patted Damon's neck. "Are you ready, boy?"

Damon snorted. He was always ready to run.

"I will call the start," Tom pulled his handkerchief from his pocket. "When the flag drops."

Addie moved her horse into position next to Mr. Eldridge, who extended his hand to her. "The winner will owe the loser one favour to be decided whenever the winner decides to call it in."

"Any favour?" She held her hand mere inches from his, hesitating to agree to such a wager until all the terms had been declared.

Mr. Eldridge nodded.

"I can trust your honour that such a favour will not ruin my reputation?"

Mr. Eldridge chuckled. "You may. May I trust the same of you?"

Addie smirked. "Most likely. A gentleman's reputation is far more difficult to ruin, after all."

When was the last time she had felt so light that she would tease anyone, especially a handsome gentleman, about such things?

"Are the terms acceptable to you? They are to me." Mr. Eldridge's hand was still hanging in the air in front of her.

With a smile and a flutter of anticipation, Addie placed her hand in his and gave it a firm shake.

Then, leaning forward, she whispered "take to the skies" to Damon just as she always did before they set off for a good run.

Chapter 2

Most likely? She would most likely keep his reputation intact? Robert could not help but chuckle at the impertinent reply. Miss Atwood seemed as lively as her mount, which, after a whisper from his rider, was snorting and ready to run.

Robert's eyes swept up and down the lady beside him. He, too, would be ready to do whatever she asked if she were to lean into him like that or put her lovely lips near his ear to say anything. She could be scolding him for all he cared, as long as she was so intently focused on him as she was her horse. Was there anything more beguiling than a female perched on the back of a fine mount?

"Eldridge."

Robert turned his eyes toward Tom, who waved his handkerchief and smirked.

"Are you ready?"

There was laughter underscoring the words.

"Yes, of course. Get on with it," Robert replied, as heat crept up his neck at having been caught admiring his challenger. But how could he not admire her? She was a golden beauty.

The flag fell, and before Robert could think to spur his horse into action, Miss Atwood was a length ahead of him. For the brief amount of time it took for Robert to register that he was falling behind before he had even begun, the question of what favour Miss Atwood would claim as her prize flitted through his mind. Pushing such a delicious contemplation aside, Robert turned his focus to the race, folding forward to nearly lay on Hugo's neck and taking care to remain seated as he had promised he would.

A half-length.

His companion lifted and lowered very prettily with her horse's gait.

A quarter length.

Though her head did not turn to check his progress, she tapped Damon's haunches with her cane and appeared to press herself forward as if she sensed how near Robert was to overtaking her.

Only a head separated him from the lead.

Her hand which held the crossed reins pumped in and out on Damon's neck. She was a frightfully impressive rider. So good, in fact, that it was tempting to stop urging Hugo forward just so he could watch her ride. However, he did not, and with two more strides, he gained the lead, though just. It was a pity that he could no longer see her.

He glanced over his shoulder as the fence approached. She was not slowing.

"Up, boy," she called. "Over."

She was going to take the fence. Robert pressed Hugo forward. It would be best if he was across the gate before she attempted it. Hugo lifted into the air and landed only seconds before Damon landed beside him.

Both he and Miss Atwood gradually brought their horses to a walk, circling back toward the fence, where their friends had joined them.

Miss Atwood offered him her hand when they had finally stopped in front of the fence.

"Hugo is the best," she said with a smile, one eyebrow cocking up as he took her hand and shook it, "today," she added.

Robert chuckled. "Just today?"

She nodded and gave her hand a tiny tug, reminding him to release it, though he ignored her.

"Does that mean I will have to prove his greatness again on some other day?"

She shrugged and smiled. "I make no such promises."

She was delightfully full of spirit.

"I will look forward to the challenge." He gave her hand one last shake and released it.

"What is your favour?" she asked.

Robert shook his head. "I have no idea, but I will claim it at some point."

"Were you wagering with a lady?" Faith scolded.

"Yes." Robert looked at his sister. "And she wagered with me. It was a fair agreement."

"As it should be," Faith retorted. "And it is about time you started treating ladies with such respect."

"When have I not –" He ceased speaking and his eyes narrowed as Faith grinned. She was baiting him.

"It was a very well-run race," Miss Price inserted. "I should not be sorry to watch such a race again."

"I would not be opposed to running it again," Robert assured her. Miss Price was also a pretty young lady, but as much as he had enjoyed playing cards with her at Mansfield, she was far more obliging than Robert would wish for in a future mate. He was quite used to his sister's liveliness, and he feared growing bored if he did not marry a lady with some spirit. His eyes turned once again to Miss Atwood. A lady such as Miss Atwood was would do quite well as a partner for his future life, and it would be no hardship to ponder the idea.

"Another day, perhaps," that lady replied. "Maybe this time with a few others to add to the excitement?"

"I would join you," Miss Price said, "but I know I could never win."

"Never say never." Miss Atwood smiled sweetly at Miss Price.

They must be good friends. That was a good sign, for

then, he might often get to be in company with Miss Atwood while he was at Mansfield.

"I could instruct you on some techniques," Miss Atwood offered.

"I should like to be included in that," Faith inserted. "I have yet to come as close to beating Robert as you have."

"No," Robert answered. "That is a very bad idea."

"Why is that?" Miss Atwood walked her horse through the gate, which Edmund had opened.

"I must be allowed to have one thing at which I am better than my sister," Robert said as they began their ride back toward Mansfield.

Tom guffawed at that while Faith and the others only chuckled. But then, Tom had heard Robert's complaints about his sister's scolding and prodding more than anyone else had.

Faith was smart and determined. Much like a rod of iron in a smithy's hands, her will took a great deal of work to bend. She and Robert were only at Mansfield because she had finally met with the one thing which seemed able to sway her with an ease like nothing else ever had, and that force was Tom Bertram, the fellow who was now leaning toward her and saying something which caused her to smile. Oh, it was good to see her so happy.

"A penny for your thoughts?"

Robert turned from his contemplation of his sister to find Miss Atwood riding beside him.

"I was merely considering how happy my sister is."
There was no need to hide such a thing. He did not care
who knew that he was a bit sentimental when it came to
his older sister. She had been the closest thing he had to a
mother for several years now.

"She does look it."

"Do you have any sisters?"

She shook her head. "Just one brother. He is nearly
done with his studies."

"Ah." There was something in how she answered which
made Robert suspect she either was not entirely happy
with the fact that her brother was her brother or the fact
that he was soon finishing school. He would have to ask
Tom about that later. "And are your parents pleased with
his progress?"

"Father is, but we no longer have a mother."

"Nor do I." He favoured her with a sad smile. "However,
I also no longer have a father. In fact, Faith is the sum total
of my family."

"Then it is good she is so well-loved by you."

Out of the corner of his eye, he saw her pull herself
straight.

"I fear my lot will not be so happy when my father
passes," she added.

He shot her a curious look.

"He is ill." She glanced at him before turning her eyes

forward and adding, "Apoplexy. He may survive as he is for some time or..."

Not long at all. The unspoken words hung in the air like a fog covering the depths of a valley, thick and oppressive.

Not long at all seemed to be a common state of being for the heads of estates in the area – or, at least, the two of whom Robert knew.

"We must always hope for the best."

"And prepare for the worse," she added.

Her comment reminded him of his sister. "My sister is good at making preparations to ward against an uncertain future. She had put aside a tidy sum of money before the fire at Mansfield, for she was resolute that her destiny would never be outside of her power to see happy – or, more specifically, her future would never be wanting."

They rode silently for a distance.

"Why did you say before the fire at Mansfield? Does she not have her money any longer?"

The question made him smile. Miss Atwood was inquisitive. He had suspected she was. He enjoyed ladies who were so and who were not afraid to inquire about things that interested them.

"She discovered that her future would always be wanting without Bertram." He left his answer there, hoping to taunt her into asking further.

Once again, it took a few strides of their horses before she spoke.

"But what of her money?"

"Tom needed money to repair the damaged wing of the house, and to do so, he was unable to continue in a financial venture. My sister has a sizable dowry which will aid in the repairs to Mansfield and the money, which she had earned in investments, she reallocated to the venture that Tom had been forced to abandon."

"Indeed?" There was a note of awe in Miss Atwood's tone. "Your sister knows about investments?"

Robert nodded.

"And you do not mind that she does?"

Robert shook his head.

"Do you take her advice?"

"Not without argument," he replied with a smile.

She laughed. "But you do think she is capable of giving good advice, do you not?"

The answer to the question seemed most important based on how she was looking at him so intently.

"You must not tell her this, but I do not *think* she is capable of giving good advice. I *know* she is."

Oh, heavens! There was something more beguiling than a beautiful woman perched on horseback, and that was a beautiful woman, who could nearly outrace him, perched on the back of a magnificent steed and smiling at him as if he had said the most wonderful thing ever. Not that he knew what he had said which was so brilliant.

"Do you wish for me to ride with you?" Miss Price

inserted herself into the conversation before Robert could attempt to discover why Miss Atwood seemed so pleased with him.

"No, no. The stable is not far from here."

"Are you certain you do not wish for me to see you home?" Miss Price asked.

"Absolutely certain," Miss Atwood replied. "For if you do, then who shall see you home?"

Robert thought of offering his services.

"I shall be home before you have even reached Mansfield's grove." She turned to Robert. "It has been a pleasure to meet you, Mr. Eldridge. I do hope I have the good fortune of seeing you again in the future."

"As do I," Robert replied.

"Would you be so kind as to extend my pleasure to your sister?"

"Of course," he answered.

"Then I will bid you a good day." She leaned over and grasped Miss Price's hand. "Until tomorrow, unless it rains."

"Oh, I hope it does not," Miss Price cried, and Robert had to agree that rain would be a very bad thing if it meant not seeing Miss Atwood.

"Do send word to Silverthorne if Mrs. Bertram needs anything," she said to Edmund. "I know that you have relations at Mansfield. However, I would like to be of service, and you are all occupied with Sir Thomas and the fire."

"And you have your father," Edmund said softly.

"He would understand. Please?"

Edmund nodded. "Very well, I will send word should there be any need of which Fanny thinks you should be made aware."

Miss Atwood did not seem pleased with that response. "Susan, you will send for me, will you not?"

Edmund chuckled. "We will not ignore you. And I will extend your wishes to Fanny for her health."

Miss Atwood thanked him, and then, turning her horse to the right, bent forward, and whispered "take to the skies" just loudly enough for Robert to catch it, and Damon was off, pounding his way across the land, his head, as well as his rider, bobbing up and down rhythmically as if one.

It was a mesmerizing sight, which held Robert captive until Edmund called his name. He really needed to do a better job of not appearing so fond of the Bertram's neighbour if he ever wished either Bertram brother to stop smirking at him.

Chapter 3

Just before reaching the paddock next to the stables, Addie slowed Damon to a walk. He needed to cool down, and she was in no hurry to face the rest of the day. She could not remember when she had enjoyed a more pleasant morning ride. Mr. Eldridge was certainly handsome. He was also a brilliant rider, but not so much of an expert as to think himself always the best. Had he not complimented her on her riding? The thought caused her lips to curl into a satisfied smile.

Added to his pleasing features and his ability to ride, was the fact that Mr. Eldridge was not the sort to think a female was stupid just because she was a female, for he not only approved of his sister's knowing about investments, he thought she was capable of giving good advice. And that last fact was likely his most attractive feature. How lovely it must be to be thought capable of more than running a household and hosting soirees with aplomb.

James had thought that way about her at one time — before he had gone to school. Her father assured her that it was just a stage of life, a place where James would find himself and learn what he needed to be a gentleman who could form his own opinions based on a broad base of experiences. However, Addie was not so certain, and even if it was just a season, this season was a painful one. She missed her sensible and caring brother, and she was fearful he was gone from her forever, much as her father might soon be.

Reluctantly, she rounded the stables and prepared to go about the business of seeing to the running of her father's house.

"Ah, there he is."

"James? What are you doing here?" Her brother was standing beside a rather well-dressed gentleman of about forty. It was not anyone she had ever seen before, and from the way the man's eyes roved her figure with appreciation, he was not someone she ever wished to see again.

"I am just showing this gent a horse."

Addie looked to her right and left. There were presently no horses in the yard.

"What horse?" She handed her reins to a groom and stepped down onto the mounting steps next to which she had stopped.

"Why Damon, of course."

Damon? Addie stood frozen to the top step, her hand resting in that of a groom who was to help see her safely to the ground.

"He is the finest gelding we have and an excellent racer."

"He is also mine," Addie inserted. Father had given Damon to her four years ago.

"He is part of our stables," James retorted with a glare which spoke loudly of his not wishing for her to say anything further.

"He is mine," she said through clenched teeth as she finally descended the steps.

"Not if Mr. Camden and I can come to a reasonable arrangement."

She would see about that. She turned away from James, gave a few brief instructions to the groom who held her horse, and, with her chin lifted, walked past her brother and toward the house. Surely, Father would not allow Robert to sell Damon.

This was just more proof that the brother who cared for her was gone. She brushed at tears as she walked toward the house. Surely, Father would not approve of selling Damon. Surely, he would not.

~*~*~

"Let me tell you again," Addie said to her father twenty minutes later. He did not seem shocked by her revelation. Perhaps he had not understood what she had said.

"James has a gentleman at the stables and is –" She stopped when her father tapped the table behind which he sat.

"I... know... My mind... works."

So he knew? And he did nothing to stop James? Her heart sank and threatened to crumble. "But Father, Damon is mine. You gave him to me."

The left side of her father's mouth twitched, and his eyes grew sad. "It is..." She could see that he was attempting to search his mind for a word and make his mouth form it.

Do not say necessary, she begged silently. *Do not say necessary.* Her heartbeat drummed in her ears as she waited.

"Necess... necessary," he finally finished his thought just as she dreaded he would.

"Why? What has James done?" She shook her head. That was a foolish question with an obvious answer. "He owes that man something, doesn't he?"

Her father's head nodded awkwardly. "He is... dangerous." His hand reached out for her. "You... will... marry and then... you will not need..." Again, his lips twisted as he fought to form the word. "Damon."

She would always need Damon for she had no intention of marrying a gentleman who would not allow her to ride. Therefore, Damon would be needed. He was her horse, and a precious gift from a beloved father, whom she had always thought had understood her. But perhaps he did not.

However, marriage was not even a possibility at present.

"How will I ever marry when I cannot enter society as a proper young lady should? I cannot leave you, and even if

I could, James is not capable of seeing to my future." She huffed and sank down in a chair next to her father as she took the hand her father had extended to her. "If there was ever any doubt, he is dispelling that right now." She shook her head as tears formed in her eyes.

"I... have a... friend."

"No, Father, no. I am not marrying Mr. Northcott. No."

Mr. Northcott was nearly fifty! And he was rather round and adored drinking enough to cause his cheeks to be perpetually red and his humor to be overbearingly, and often, nonsensically, jubilant. She did not care if the man also had a healthy fortune and a fine estate. Nor did she care that her father had known him for years. There was no way she was going to willingly be Mr. Northcott's wife and bear his children. The mere thought caused her stomach to roil and her skin to crawl.

"James has... friends."

"Who are as inept and stupid as he is!" There was not a one among them whom she would consider as an acceptable match – for anyone, let alone, herself.

"Adela." The stroke had not removed her father's ability to say her name in a scolding tone.

"I apologize. That was unkind." And true. Excessively, frustratingly true! "He is selling my horse. My horse," she whispered as the tears she had been fighting won the battle and flowed freely down her cheeks.

Her father squeezed her hand, and she returned the gesture. Not because she wished to tell him that she loved him – she did, of course — she just did not feel like saying it right now. However, she also knew that she did not have the luxury to withhold such words even when angry and hurt, for she did not know how many more times she would be able to say them and did not wish to regret having withheld them if her father should not survive until she was feeling more loved and loving.

She lifted the hand which held hers and kissed it. Then, she rose to retire to her room where she could wallow in her heartbreak alone.

Her father, however, did not immediately let go of her hand. "Your aunt..."

She shook her head. She had no desire to have her aunt help her find a husband. Aunt Edith's idea of a proper husband would likely not take into account the state of the man's stables.

"I cannot leave you. I will not." She bent and kissed his forehead.

He held her hand tightly. "It is... arranged."

"What is arranged?" What was he talking about? Did he even know? There were times when his mind became muddled.

He shook his head. "Ask Mr. Fulton."

She nodded her understanding. To explain was presently too much for him. However, his man of business knew the particulars.

"I will," she assured him. "Do you wish to go to bed? You look tired."

Again, he shook his head. "I am... sorry."

"About what?"

"Damon."

His voice was weak, and, like it or not, she was going to send someone to inquire about his returning to bed. She would wait a few minutes, but within half an hour, she hoped he would be resting on his pillows instead of sitting by the table in his room attempting to write things out with a hand that only half worked.

"Addie?"

She turned towards him from the doorway.

"I love you." He rarely slurred those words, and he always managed a beautiful smile when he said them. It was as if they worked a magic in him which nothing else could.

"And I love you." She blew him a kiss as she had always done since she was a little girl, and he with a somewhat stiff hand caught it and pressed it to his heart.

Half an hour later, Addie's father was back in his bed, but he was not resting. At least, he was not resting how Addie had wished for him to rest. He had been insensible when his man had found him, slumped over his table, his pen still in his hand. The surgeon had been called, but there was nothing they could do but wait to see if he would regain his senses and, only when he did, would they know the full extent of the damage done.

"You came to see him about Damon." James's voice was accusatory when he stopped her outside their father's room.

She had just been sent out of the room by Mr. Sydney, the surgeon.

"Yes, I saw him." She shoved his hand away from her arm. Her nerves were in no condition to tolerate her brother's scolding. Their father could be dying, and he was concerned that she had gone to their father about his selling a horse — her horse? "He gave me Damon."

"I know." He attempted to snatch her arm again, but she pulled it way. "I remember the day quite well. It was just a few days before I left for school." He followed her down the hall as she walked away from him.

"How could you, James?" She whirled on him and did not even attempt to keep the hurt she felt out of her voice. "Do you truly care for me so little?"

His head snapped backward, and he looked both shocked and affronted. "What do you mean, do I care for you so little? You are my sister. Of course, I care for you."

Addie folded her arms and blinked at the tears which were once again forming their battle lines. Her nose and eyes would be permanently swollen and red before this day was through. And to think that it had started out so well.

"Do you really?" she snapped.

"It is a horse, Addie," he cried in exasperation. "I will get you another as soon as I am able."

"It was a gift from Father. How can you replace that?"

He grabbed her elbow and moved her down the hall to her room from where they had been standing near their father's door. He pushed her inside the room and closed the door behind him.

"Would you rather I sell you to Mr. Camden?"

Addie staggered backward a pace. "I beg your pardon?"

"Mr. Camden has been known to extract his displeasure at not being paid in beatings, or worse." James stood in front of the door, his shoulders lifting and lowering in a noticeable fashion. "And to collect his payment by selling gentlemen's female folk at brothels."

Addie was certain her eyes were about to pop out of her head and roll across the floor. She blinked just to ensure they stayed inside her head. "How did you become involved with a man like that?"

James ran a hand through his hair. "It was not purposefully done. I thought I could win. I had never been to this place before but had heard from Willet that it was the place to make a fortune in one night."

How stupid was he? "And you believed that?"

He shrugged. "I had been drinking."

Of course, he had! "James."

"I know. I know. I have been attempting to get the

money together to give to Camden, but I simply could not get enough. So, I offered him a prize gelding." He crossed and took Addie by the shoulders. "I know it was not right to promise him your horse. I know that you might forever hate me, but I had heard him talking to someone who mentioned to him that I had a sister. He seemed quite interested in that fact in a way in which I would not care to share with you."

Horror thick as molasses on a cold winter's day settled in Addie's chest. Did her brother ever think things all the way through before acting?

"And you brought him here?"

James nodded. "To see the horse. He seemed interested in it and said he was willing to strike a deal if the horse was to his liking."

"And if it is not?"

The fear Addie felt finally registered in her brother's eyes. "I will see him to an inn by pleading Father's illness as the reason."

"Will that not offend him?" She could go to Mansfield. She would be safe there. However, she would also be away from her father, and she could not leave him. Not now.

"I will attempt it. What else can I do?"

"Oh, James, you can start contemplating the ramifications of your actions before you find yourself in such a quandary as this."

Her brother released his grip on her shoulders and,

turning away, ran his hand through his hair again. "I have made a grand mess of things, have I not?" He shook his head. "I have been attempting to right things for months. I assure you, Addie, that I am not the same fool I was. I am a slightly wiser one."

Addie sighed. Arguing with him over his amount of stupidity was not going to change a thing. Damon had to be sold in order to keep both herself and her brother safe.

"See what can be done. You did not plan for Father to be ill. Hopefully, Mr. Camden will understand that, but whatever you do, do not meet with him alone. Always have someone near, if not in, the room. I am angry with you, but I do not wish to see you beaten." She sank down on the edge of her bed. "And James?"

He turned towards her.

"I will do my best to convince Mr. Camden of Damon's value." She gave him a half-smile. "I suppose keeping a brother is better than keeping a horse. But do not think for one moment that I will let you forget this any time soon."

"I have no doubt of that."

"I fully intend to act put out that you are taking such a fine horse from me, and if Mr. Camden is as vile as you say, he might find the prize more appealing if he knows it will harm someone." She leveled a glare at her brother. "Which it will."

He closed his eyes and nodded. There appeared to be some of her former loving brother behind the pain etched into his features at her comment. He had not lost all care for her.

"If there had been any other way, Addie," he whispered.

"There is just one more thing, and I will see to informing the staff." She blew out a breath. "If Father should die, no one must know until Mr. Camden has left. If he knows you have inherited, he might push for more."

"How did my little sister become so smart?"

Despite the gravity of their current situation, Addie smiled to hear him call her smart. "We have both been taking lessons, big brother. It is just that I have been receiving an education in the running of an estate while you have been gaining an education in how not to gamble."

Chapter 4

"What was that about?" Robert was standing at the foot of the stairs down which the surgeon, who had been calling on Sir Thomas, had raced.

"It seems Mr. Atwood is in need of urgent attention." Tom shook his head and looked up the stairs he had just descended. "I cannot imagine how Addie is handling all of this. I am struggling with my father being incapacitated, but I have Mother and Faith as well as Susan, you, and Edmund and Fanny. Miss Atwood has no one. Her brother is still at school." Tom shook his head once again. "I cannot fathom having to face this and care for a sister." He clapped Robert on the shoulder. "You have not done things perfectly, but you have done well."

"Faith has done well," Robert replied. "I would have been a far greater mess without her to badger me into doing what needed doing."

Miss Atwood's comments about her brother came to mind. "Is there something amiss between Miss Atwood and her brother?"

Tom's brow furrowed.

"She did not seem pleased when speaking of him earlier. The implication was that he did not care for her, and she did not seem happy with him or with his almost being done school. I was not sure which it was."

Tom shrugged. "I am not certain. I know they got on well when they were younger." He stepped toward the drawing room. "Susan," he called and then waited for her to join him in the gallery.

"Did you need something?" Susan asked when she had joined them.

"I have some news which you will wish to know. However, I wonder if you might, first, answer a question for Mr. Eldridge."

"Of course."

"How do Addie and James get on?" Tom asked.

Susan looked between them. Her eyes clearly saying she was not certain how to answer such a question or if she even should.

"It was something she said earlier which made me think she and her brother do not get along well," Robert explained. "I am being too nosy by half."

"I could not give him an answer," Tom added. "I have been away so much that I do not know." He smiled sadly. "That was not very well done on my part."

"You will not share this?" Susan asked quietly with a look back toward the drawing room.

"No," both Tom and Robert answered together.

"James has changed since he left for school. He treats her as if she knows nothing." She pulled the corner of her bottom lip between her teeth and looked at the floor. "She has not said it as such, but I believe he prefers his friends to his family."

Tom closed his eyes and blew out a breath. Robert knew that such a statement hit close to home for his friend, and he suspected from the "my apologies" whispered by Susan, she also knew how much such a statement would be felt by Tom.

"Then, this news will be even harder to share and hear," Tom said. "I am certain a letter will arrive for you soon enough, but the surgeon was called away to Silverthorne just now. It seems Mr. Atwood has had another seizure. The worst so far." He wrapped his cousin in his arms when she gasped and looked faint. "I think it might be good if we were to pay a visit to Addie. Just to see if there is anything she needs. Would you like to do that?"

"Oh, yes, but have you finished what you needed to do with Edmund?"

Tom squeezed his cousin tight. "Yes, Susie, I have. Now, are you well enough to get ready?"

Susan nodded.

"Then, I will tell my mother that we are going out and see if I can coax Miss Eldridge into accompanying us." He smiled for he knew, as well as Robert did, that if there was a person whom Faith knew who was in trouble, she would be amongst the first to lend her aid. In fact, the person did not have to be known to Faith if that person fell into her realm and needed care. That was how Tom had been saved after his fall.

~*~*~

Half an hour later, the four of them, Faith, Susan, Robert, and Tom, were sitting in Tom's carriage on their way to Silverthorne. Edmund had been persuaded to go home to his wife with the assurance that if his services as parson were needed, he would be called for directly. And Susan had also promised to inform him of all she knew when Tom stopped at the parsonage on their way home.

Half an hour after entering the carriage, the party from Mansfield exited it and entered Silverthorne Court.

"James, I did not realize you were at home," Tom said in surprise when they were shown to the drawing room. "Mr. Camden." Tom greeted the wiry looking fellow next to Tom before glancing at Robert.

They both knew who Mr. Camden was. Things could not be good if Mr. James Atwood was in the company of Mr. Camden.

"Bertram, Eldridge," Camden greeted them as if this were his drawing room and not that of Mr. Atwood. But then, that was how Camden was. He took possession of anywhere and anything that he wished. And woe be to the fellow who opposed him.

ADDIE: TO WAGER ON HER FUTURE

"We came to see if Miss Atwood needed assistance. The surgeon was at Mansfield," Tom explained succinctly.

Robert knew that his friend was keeping as much information to himself as possible. One did not give away details to a man like Camden. A friend of theirs had run afoul of him once, and, to this day, that friend walked with a limp from the damage Camden's thugs had done to him. Truth be told, he was fortunate to be walking at all.

"My sister is upstairs in her room," James said. "She is understandably overwhelmed by all that has happened. I was just offering to escort Mr. Camden to the Red Lion. I am certain there would be far better entertainment there than at a house where its inhabitants are so distracted by grave matters." He shifted uneasily and cast a wary glance at Camden.

Good. Young Atwood seemed to have enough sense to wish to see Camden gone as soon as could be managed.

"I hear," Tom said, "that there is still a bit of a special guests game played there a few nights of the week. This might be one of them."

Camden's eyes lit at that information.

"There are not very many deep pockets here, but it could prove diverting," Tom added.

"Will either of you be there?" Camden's smile was a sickeningly rapacious as Robert remembered it.

"No. I am afraid we have thrown off such frivolities in

favour or a more genteel and boring existence," Robert quipped.

"And do these ladies have anything to do with this change of habit?"

Robert shook his head. "No, not a thing." It was a lie. Faith was a large part of his giving up of his former life. However, he was not about to share the identity of his sister or Miss Price with the man. And so far, they had managed to avoid any introductions.

"Addie would be pleased to see you in the blue drawing room," James inserted. He looked at Susan. "I believe you know the way?"

She nodded.

"I will return as quickly as I can." James waved his arm towards the door in invitation for Mr. Camden to exit in front of him.

"There is no need for you to leave your guests, Atwood. I am certain there must be a groom who can show me the way. Perhaps one who knows your horses well and can tell me if there are any others in which I might be interested." His brows rose. "I am not about to settle on the first one you show me."

The words were said pleasantly, but there was a steeliness to the man's eyes. Robert would put a hundred pounds on Mr. James Atwood being in debt to the man. Camden only liked horses if they were taking him from one game to another or winning money for him on a track.

"I am certain I could tell you about the horses better than any groom."

"I doubt that," Camden said. "If I am to talk to any Atwood about horses, I think it ought to be your sister. She seemed to know her way with that horse you showed me earlier. I dare say she knows more than you."

"Only because I have been at school."

"Then, it is either her or a groom," Camden said. "Take your pick."

"Very well, I am certain we can find a groom to your liking in the stables." Again, James waved his arm toward the door.

"You expect me to leave without being introduced to these lovely ladies."

"Yes," Robert answered. "They are no one to you."

Mr. Camden chuckled. "Brave words."

"They do not wish an introduction," Robert added.

Mr. Camden stepped closer to Robert and gave each lady a sweeping look. "This one is your sister. She looks too much like you to not be related," he said, indicating Faith. "And this other one is some relation of Bertram. Oh, she could be your lady, I suppose, but I do not think so. She seems a bit too skittish for you." His mouth tipped into a smirk. "Not that skittishness cannot be trained out of a filly." He winked at Susan and then, with a laugh, he exited the room.

James gave them a pleading look. "Addie is upstairs. I will return as soon as possible."

Tom grabbed James's arm. "Keep someone with you."

James nodded. "I have already promised Addie I would."

"Good. She is sensible."

Again, James nodded. "I know." He blew out a breath. "And I am not."

"There are many of us who have been less than sensible," Tom assured him. "But Eldridge and I have seen of what Camden is capable. Keep someone with you – preferably someone strong or armed." Tom tilted his head toward the door. "Do not keep him waiting. He is not a patient fellow."

James scooted from the room.

"Lead us to the blue drawing room," Tom said to Susan.

"Who is that man?" Faith whispered.

"A sharp, who I am guessing has gotten his talons into Mr. Atwood," Tom answered.

"Oh dear!" Susan cried.

"Indeed," Robert agreed as he followed Susan up the stairs and down the hall to a door on the right. To his surprise, she knocked rather than just entering.

"Addie," Susan called. "We are here to see if you need anything.

"We?" Miss Atwood said as she opened the door to what appeared to be her private sitting room and not a drawing room at all – although, it was blue.

"Oh, I see." Her eyes, which were understandably red, grew wide as she took in who was standing outside her door.

"Your brother sent us up here," Tom said. "He and Mr. Camden were just leaving."

"Mr. Camden is going to the inn, then?"

"Yes."

Miss Atwood blew out a heavy sigh. "Thank the Lord. Come in. Come in. This is the safest place to talk." She held the door open for them, and then once they were all inside, she closed that door and another door which was opened to her bedchamber.

"I am not entirely certain what to do. The surgeon is with Father now, but I do not think there is much to be done besides wait." She took a seat next to Susan, who placed an arm around her shoulder.

"And what of your brother and Mr. Camden?" Robert asked.

"I do not know the extent of what my brother owes the man, but..." She shrugged.

"They are not on friendly terms then?" Robert pressed. He suspected they were not, but he needed to know for Miss Atwood's safety was dependent upon it.

She shook her head.

"Good."

She gave him an inquisitive look.

"Bertram and I know of him."

"Is he as dangerous as my brother says?"

"Likely more so," Robert replied. Very likely more.

He settled back in his chair and listened as Susan began plying Miss Atwood with questions about her father. He glanced at Tom who was listening carefully to all that Miss Atwood said. A father on the cusp of dying was a tragedy of unequal proportions. Robert knew that full well, but then to have added to it a brother who had put himself in a tenuous position? That made it exponentially worse.

His eyes shifted to Faith, and he chided himself. Was this not what she had been attempting to tell him? His actions were not just a danger to himself and his future, but also to the happiness and safety of anyone close to him.

He watched Miss Atwood clasp and unclasp her hands while she spoke. She was naturally uneasy and likely scared. It hurt his heart to think about it, and he knew exactly how his sister felt when she visited her friend Olivia.

He would have to tell Faith later that she was right to have scolded him as she had. Oh, he knew he could keep such thoughts as he was currently thinking to himself to avoid enduring the pleasure his sister would find in his admission, but for all the grief he had given her during his days of carefree extravagance, it was truly a small penalty to pay.

Chapter 5

Of all the people lounging in her sitting room, the one who kept drawing Addie's attention was Mr. Eldridge. It was odd how she had only met him earlier in the day and yet, he seemed so at ease with her. He was likely one of those fortunate chaps who found friends wherever he was.

His smile was quick and his eyes expressive, though there were moments when such things were hidden behind an unreadable mien. That talent, she supposed, had been developed while participating in card games and whatever else he might have thrown his money at in a gamble to increase his coffers. He was Tom's friend, after all, and Tom Bertram was no saint.

She, herself, was not completely opposed to a wager now and again. However, when a wager endangered the welfare of one's self, friends, or family, it was excessively unacceptable. Life was not free of risks, but one should not throw oneself into them willy-nilly — such as her brother had done or as Tom had done in risking his inheritance and that of his brother.

She smiled at Mr. Eldridge, who was watching her, and wondered if he were the sort of gentleman who had risked where it was not wise to do so. He did not appear to be such a one. However, neither did Tom.

She rose and rang the bell. They might not be in the usual drawing room used for entertaining guests, but she could still offer them a cup of tea, and to be honest, she felt as if she could use a cup herself. The mere ritual of pouring tea and stirring in milk always calmed her, and at present, she needed calming.

Before she could return to her seat, there was a knock on her door.

"Is your brother here?" Mr. Sydney, the surgeon, asked as he peered around the room.

"Not yet," Addie answered. "How is my father?"

Mr. Sydney was another fellow who had perfected the ability to hide behind an indecipherable expression. Of course, he only did so when the news he had to share was not good. If things were well, his lips would quirk at the corners, causing his cheeks to become even rounder than they were when he was not smiling. Presently, he was not smiling.

"He is resting."

"For now?" Addie asked softly.

There was a small flinch of his left eye. "Yes."

"For how long?"

"We should wait for your brother."

"I am capable of hearing the dreadful news."

This time he smiled, though sadly at her. "I have no doubt of that, Miss Atwood, but I do not relish imparting what I must more than I must."

Addie's heart ached at the meaning of his words as she motioned to an empty chair, but her sorrow must be kept contained for the moment. She would grieve when she was in private and not entertaining guests.

"Please, be seated," she said to Mr. Sydney. "I am unsure how long my brother will be, but there is a matter of some delicacy of which you must be made aware." Precautions must be taken. She must keep her head and steady her nerves. Her safety and that of her brother depended upon it.

Mr. Sydney did as instructed but not without giving her a questioning look after his eyes had swept the room.

"Should we leave?" Mr. Eldridge asked.

Addie shook her head. "I assume you are trustworthy if you are Mr. Bertram's friend. I am not mistaken, am I?"

"No, but if it is a private matter," Mr. Eldridge replied.

"You know Mr. Camden."

Mr. Eldridge's brow furrowed. "Yes, but –"

"And you do not approve of him and are likely cautious in his presence and wary of his motives, are you not?" Someone who knew Mr. Camden might help her brother circumvent any further disastrous dealings with the man.

"You asked if my brother and he were friends and

looked relieved when I said they were not," she added when his look of confusion deepened at her question.

Understanding dawned in Mr. Eldridge's eyes. "I have seen his handiwork and let us just say that Mr. Sydney would be put to the test to see such handiwork undone if it is even possible to be undone." He took a deep breath and exhaled slowly before continuing. "If your father was not in a precarious position, I would recommend removing yourself from the house until Mr. Camden is gone."

"He is at the inn." Addie's heart picked up its pace at the silent disbelief that met her comment.

"It is what I would recommend for my sister," Mr. Eldridge finally said breaking the silence. "But then, I am rather protective of her."

Addie looked to Miss Eldridge for confirmation of such a statement.

"He has been foolish in many ways," Miss Eldridge said, "but I must admit that he has never once knowingly placed me in a dangerous situation. His friends have not always been so fortunate."

"Might we forget that I left Tom while he was injured? I do believe I have learned that lesson quite well."

So, it was Mr. Eldridge's estate where Tom had convalesced until being returned to Mansfield. That answered her question of whether Mr. Eldridge had done anything unwise. He and Mr. Bertram must be prodigiously good friends to have weathered that ordeal. And, she added to herself, both seemed to be wiser for it. There was hope that James would also be wiser once the matter with Mr. Camden was settled. That was a small comforting thought in a sea of so much uncertainty and grief.

Miss Eldridge smiled. "I suppose we can put it aside — for now."

Mr. Eldridge shook his head and turned away from his sister. "Why does my knowing Camden play into why I should interfere in a private matter?"

"You can vouchsafe for me that the gamble we are about to take is necessary."

Tom chuckled, causing Addie to look his direction.

"You sound a great deal like Miss Eldridge," Tom explained. "She only gambles when necessary."

Addie smiled at Miss Eldridge. "That seems rather wise."

She turned back to Mr. Eldridge to continue her explanation. "If Mr. Camden is as wily and dangerous as I suspect he is from what my brother said, then he must not know when or if my father dies." She pressed her lips together and willed her emotions to remain under control. Admitting the reality of her father's soon departure was not easily done with any sort of composure. However, after a moment, she resumed her explanation. "Should Mr. Camden learn that my brother has inherited, he might require more than Damon as payment."

"Damon? Your horse?" Mr. Eldridge interrupted. Disbelief was written in his wide eyes and lifted eyebrows.

"Yes, Damon is Silverthorne Hall's best. He would command the highest price at auction for his linage is beyond compare and you have seen his speed. Any gentleman, who wished to train him properly to race, would be almost guaranteed the win." Again, she paused and pressed her lips together and tamped down her emotions. "I am not pleased at the prospect of losing him, of course, but the loss of a horse is a small price to pay to keep my brother whole and myself free from any design which might take Mr. Camden's mind."

"You know of that?" surprise suffused Tom's tone.

"I do. James mentioned it."

"If you do not mind my saying so," Mr. Sydney said, "this sounds like a dreadfully precarious situation."

"You would not be wrong," she assured him. She felt as if she were sitting on the limb of a tree which had fallen and was teetering over the edge of a precipice. One foul wind in just the right direction would send both it and her plummeting into the abyss beneath her.

"Place it near the window, Maggie." She turned back from speaking to her maid.

"I know that a death cannot be hidden for long, but Mr. Camden should not remain in the area overly long." Or so she hoped. How long could it take for him to accept a horse as payment for whatever debt James had incurred?

"It seems a worthy risk," Miss Eldridge said. "I only wish you did not have to take it."

"As do I!" Susan cried.

Addie shrugged and rose to see to the pouring of the tea. "It cannot be helped." She looked at Mr. Sydney. "We will need you to continue to make calls after..." She could not say it. "Just until Mr. Camden leaves the area," she added in a strained whisper. Tears clung to her lower eyelid.

Susan was at her side in an instant and had an arm around her shoulder.

"Allow me to pour," Miss Eldridge said. "You should sit."

Addie was thankful to have someone to care for her, for she felt at the moment as if her strength had been utterly consumed. Wearily, she allowed Susan to guide her back to her chair.

"How long?" she asked Mr. Sydney once again while the tea was being poured. "Please."

The surgeon drew a breath. "I would not expect more than a week."

Though her heart was breaking, she thanked him. At least she knew. At least she could prepare herself. Not that she knew how one prepared for the loss of a parent. She had been too young to remember her mother's passing. She dabbed at those tears which were threatening to spill.

Silently, she accepted a cup of tea and drank it, slowly,

contemplating her father and her future while conversation about trivial matters took place around her. Thankfully, no one pressed her to be part of it.

Just as the empty teacups were being placed on the tray, James arrived, and after a proper introduction to Mr. Eldridge and his sister, Mr. Sydney was once again required to share his opinion on their father's health. And then, after assuring both James and Addie that he would keep their secret if the necessity arose, he left.

"I would love to visit your stables," Mr. Eldridge said in reply to James' offer once they had finished discussing the fact that Mr. Eldridge's estate was near Newmarket, which, of course, had led to a discussion about the last race either had attended. "Your sister is an excellent rider. She nearly beat me this morning."

"Did she?" James blinked. "You race?"

"Only to give Damon a chance to run as he wishes." She sighed. She would not get to do that much longer if at all.

James grimaced. "Camden might not want Damon. He has looked at three others. He seems to favour Iris."

"That cannot be done." They could not part with Iris. She was their best mare and Damon's sister. The three foals she had produced so far had all grown to be fabulously coveted and had fetched substantial money. It was due of course to her father being a prize-winning stallion. To lose her would put the estate at a disadvantage that losing a horse such as Damon would not.

"If she were with foal, he would claim her and be gone in an hour," James added.

"With two horses!" Addie cried.

"Camden is no fool when it comes to making the odds favour him," Mr. Eldridge inserted.

James blew out a breath. "If Damon were not a gelding, he might be riding him to the inn as we speak. However, upon seeing Iris, he seemed to take it into his head that a gelded horse as a racer was not as valuable to him in the future as a stallion would be. What would he do with a gelding when its career was at an end? And Damon's sire is too old for Camden's liking."

"His preference for Iris is not just as a breeder," Tom inserted. "He knows it would hurt the estate more if you lost her. He is ruthless."

"How much do you owe him?" Addie asked.

James pulled at his sleeves and looked at his boots. "Two hundred and seventy-five pounds."

Mr. Eldridge whistled. "And he is willing to take one horse for that?"

"Father gave me two hundred, and that has been paid." James rubbed the back of his neck. "It is just seventy-five remaining." He shook his head. "He offered to give me the chance to win my debt from him at the inn tonight."

"You will not attempt it, will you?" Addie's hand rested on her heart. Hopefully, James was not so foolish as to believe he had the chance to come out ahead.

James shook his head. "I plan to never wager again. Ever."

He stood and paced to the window, poured a small amount of cold tea into a cup and drank it. "He wants you to meet with him tomorrow, Addie. He seems to think you will be able to tell him more about the horses than even the groom I sent to escort him to the inn can." He shook his head and chuckled bitterly. "Though I do not doubt your knowledge of our horses, I believe it is merely because you are prettier."

"James."

"I know. Bringing him here was a mistake, as was thinking I could best him at any game of chance." Again, James rubbed the back of his neck as he looked out the window. "I just want him gone as soon as possible and my family secure."

"Then, let us make a party of it," Mr. Eldridge offered. "I should like to see the stables as I might be looking to add to my own – not in reality, but as we shall present it to Mr. Camden. If Miss Atwood is the expert, then I wish to be shown the options by her. Just tell me which horses would be those with which you would be willing to part."

Tom nodded. "That is brilliant, for if you seem interested in any in particular, he will desire that horse more."

Robert tapped his nose. "He knows I would not favour a horse of low quality for he has lost money by betting against my horses on more than one occasion."

"Must I be the voice of reason?" Miss Eldridge asked.

Addie shook her head. "No, allow me."

Miss Eldridge smiled and waved her hand as if giving the floor to Addie.

"If Mr. Camden suspects at any point that you are attempting to swindle him, things will turn from the disaster they are now to something far worse. Let me show you the horses but be honest about your assessment. I do not wish to part with any of them, but if you feel you must promote one horse over the rest..."

She squared her shoulders and swallowed her sorrow. There would be other horses. She would demand Iris's next foal. "Let it be Damon. Mr. Camden would not be disappointed with him. Damon can win a race. You know he can, Mr. Eldridge."

"But he is yours," Mr. Eldridge protested.

"And Silverthorne is my home, and James is my brother. I think I should like to keep them more." She held Mr. Eldridge's gaze until finally, his shoulders drooped in a great exhalation. For being an amiable fellow, he was not without a dose of obstinacy. However, in this dispute, she had to be the victor.

"Very well," Mr. Eldridge replied, admitting his defeat and not looking at all pleased about it. "I will give an honest assessment and if I see no other horse which is better, I shall make an offer on Damon, which, in turn, will make Camden desire him."

Chapter 6

"The chestnut moves very well." Robert stood between Miss Atwood and Mr. Camden the next day, watching as Silverthorne's grooms gave several horses a gallop around the paddock. He grimaced, which was not entirely a part of his ruse. He was sorry to find that Miss Atwood had indeed been correct. Damon appeared to be the best Silverthorne had to offer. It was due, of course, to the efforts of the lady to whom he must declare his decision — a lady who did not deserve the hand being dealt her by her brother's foolishness. His conscience, thanks to Faith's dutiful scolding over the past year, pricked him.

"I know you favour him, Miss Atwood, but I should very much like to make you an offer."

"Your estate breeds horses, Eldridge," Camden inserted. "You'll not get one foal from that fellow."

"My estate also makes a good showing at the races in Newmarket, and that gelding would bring home a prize along with the recognition such a feat necessarily brings with it. And that, in turn, would make my horses and their breeding services more desirable."

Camden laughed. "You are not home enough to make any great return on such notoriety, and you will not be until you decide to start breeding your own lot."

"Which is not so far into the future," Robert hedged.

"Indeed? And does the amorous Mr. Eldridge have his eye on any lady in particular?" Camden scoffed.

"You will know when the announcement is printed in the Times," Robert retorted. As if he was going to tell the likes of Camden about any lady – real or imagined – whom he might be planning to marry.

Camden huffed. "I still think a breeder would do you better."

"And why, pray tell, are you so generously giving me your advice? Is it because you would rather have that horse – what was his name?" He turned toward James.

"Damon," James replied.

"Is it because you would rather have Damon and leave me with the scraps?"

"None of our horses are scraps." Miss Atwood's tone was as annoyed as Robert had hoped it would be. He needed Camden to believe that he and Miss Atwood were merely acquaintances.

"My apologies. I did not mean to imply any of your live-stock was inferior in any way. I was simply making the point that Damon appears to be the best in your stable."

"He is," she replied confidently.

"It is a pity he cannot sire any offspring," Camden muttered.

"He was promised to me by my father before we knew how spirited he would be," Miss Atwood explained.

"A gift from your father, you say?" Camden's interest in Damon had just risen if his tone of voice was any indicator. "It would be difficult to part with such a prized horse, especially now."

"It would be difficult at any time," Miss Atwood replied.

Robert knew it to be true. He had seen the connection Miss Atwood had with her horse. Such a friendship between rider and beast was not easily cast away.

"Then, why even put him among the lot?" Of course, Robert knew why, but Camden was not supposed to know that.

"It is not my decision." She leveled a displeased look at her brother, which, to Robert's way of thinking, the fellow well deserved.

Camden chuckled. "The sorry lot of the fairer sex. If you give him to me, you can ride him whenever you come to call."

"And why would my sister ever call on you?" James blurted.

Camden shrugged. "One never knows, but I would not turn her away if she did call." His eyes swept Miss

Atwood's figure. "She might find she grows lonely for her mount."

"It is only a horse. There will be others."

From the way her cheeks flushed, Robert was certain Miss Atwood understood the double entendre Camden had used. The old goat had been taking every opportunity to be near Miss Atwood – too near her if you were to ask Robert, which was why he was now standing between the two of them. No lady needed to be subjected to Camden's lecherous ways.

"Perhaps that is why you are so interested in that horse, Eldridge," Camden continued. "You are hoping to use it to sway Miss Atwood to your cause in filling your nurseries."

"I do not need to buy a horse to win a wife," Robert retorted, although it was not an entirely unworthy thought. If he actually could buy Damon — which he knew was not a very likely thing — he could then find a way to see Damon returned to Miss Atwood, and he would not be opposed to her visiting Stonegate to see her horse. Or, he cast a sidelong glance at Miss Atwood, it would not be a horrible thing to have her as his wife.

"However," he continued, "an alliance between Silverthorne's stables and my own would not be a bad thing. Just imagine the stock we could produce, Atwood. Why Camden here would have no choice but to bet on our horses at every race." That ought to make the fellow disquieted enough to pursue a purchase of Damon.

"My horses are for sale, gentlemen. My sister is not," James said. "The day is growing late for those who might need to travel. Could we come to a decision?"

"I would like the chestnut – Damon," Robert said. "I will give you sixty pounds for him."

"We will not part with him for less than seventy-five," James replied.

"Which is exactly what I have to offer," Camden said, stepping around Robert and extending his hand to James.

"Perhaps I can come up on my offer somewhat," Robert inserted. It would not be natural for a fellow to just give up on what he wanted without a bit of effort being thrown behind his negotiation.

"I offered first," Camden said.

"And if I were to raise the price to eighty?"

Camden shrugged. "Then I would have to settle on the mare I saw yesterday. She seems a good breeder."

Robert laughed. "You? A breeder of horses?" He laughed again. "It is a costly venture, and you would be wagering against nature." Robert shook his head in disbelief. "Your funds for the amusements to which you are accustomed would be severely curtailed. Trust me. I know."

"Then you take the breeder," Camden offered.

Robert shook his head. "I have no need for another mare, not even one with that horse's pedigree."

"Ah, but she could produce a horse that is finer than that chestnut."

"And it would be years before I could race him. Years of expenses instead of purses."

Camden's face grew hard. "I want that horse." His words were simple but unscored with a pointed look at James.

"But Mr. Eldridge has offered more," Miss Atwood inserted.

"Your brother understands that my offer has certain advantages to it which cannot be valued in sterling, my dear."

"I do not understand." Miss Atwood was playing her part of innocent sister quite well.

"Of course, you do not, my dear. These are masculine affairs and not the sort of thing your sex understands."

Robert watched Miss Atwood carefully. He was certain that such a statement would make her bristle. It would his sister, and he doubted Miss Atwood, who had been helping with the running of the estate, would take such an insult with any great equanimity. He was not wrong. Her eyes narrowed as she clenched her jaw, but she held her tongue – likely with great effort.

"Sell me the horse, Atwood, and then, Eldridge, if you wish, you can make me an offer."

"Which you will refuse," Robert retorted. "How much does Atwood owe you? Perhaps I will cover it and then buy the horse at a reduced price."

"Owe you?" Miss Atwood blinked. Her feigned look of ignorance was really quite good. "I do not understand."

"As I said, my dear, these are things for us men to discuss. You have done your part in showing us the horse quite well." He turned to Robert. "A hundred pounds."

"My brother owes you a hundred pounds?"

"No, he does not," James cried. "It is seventy-five. I owe him seventy-five pounds."

"For what?" Miss Atwood demanded.

"I lost a game," James kept his voice low as if he did not wish for her to hear him.

"A bet? I am selling my horse – a gift from our father – over a bet that you were stupid enough to make?"

Robert was almost certain that the anger Miss Atwood's voice contained was not fabricated. She had every reason to be furious over the loss of her animal because of her brother's foolishness. However, whether the anger was real or not, it was having the desired effect on Camden as his lips had curled into a pleased grin. Knowing that he had caused pain to his victims was always something that brought enjoyment to a depraved gentleman such as Camden.

"Yes, he is, my dear. Now, if you would have your groom prepare him to travel unless Eldridge wishes to give me a thousand pounds for him."

"A thousand pounds!" Miss Atwood cried.

"That does seem exorbitant," Robert said, keeping his tone calm.

"If he is as good as you have led me to believe," there was a glint of calculation in Camden's eye, "then, you know he can earn that sort of money."

Robert crossed his arms and smirked. "Not if he races my horse. I think you remember how good my horse is, do you not?"

Camden shrugged. "I remember he was better than a lot of other horses, but not this one. You said yourself that Damon is a winner. Are you willing to prove that you were not swindling me just so you could be rid of me and then purchase the horse which is truly the best in this stable?"

"I am no fool," Robert said. "I would never attempt to cheat you."

"Well, that is good to hear, but I have yet to hear if you are willing to back your expertise or not."

Robert shook his head. "I do not have a thousand pounds to wager on a race."

"But you do have a horse. A very fine horse."

"With which I have no desire to part." Though the man before him was standing still, Robert had the distinct impression that he was being circled by a ravenous wolf.

"Then, prove your value by riding Damon for me, and if he wins, I will know you were being honest and will give you a hundred pounds for your effort. However, if he loses, I will require your horse or a thousand pounds."

"No, I am not being a part of any game you are playing."

"I am not playing a game." The man's grin stood in opposition to his claim. "You realize, of course, that should you refuse my offer to ride Damon and decide, instead, to ride in a race against him and win, I will count you as a cheat." His features grew hard. "And you know how I loathe a cheat."

"You wish for Mr. Eldridge to throw a race?" Miss Atwood asked incredulously.

"Or never to enter," Mr. Camden.

"Ever? Any race?" Miss Atwood looked positively horrified.

Camden nodded.

"But if he rides Damon and wins, then, he can ride against Damon in the future?" Miss Atwood shook her head as if comprehending Camden was no easy task — which to anyone with even a partially working moral compass, it was not.

"Only if Damon wins."

"Damon is the best horse in our stables," James said. "I have told you that time and again."

"Yes, but you are attempting to save your neck. You would say anything," Camden said dismissively.

"But it is true!" Miss Atwood cried. "Damon is the fastest horse we have, and I am not eager to part with him. Therefore, you can believe me."

"I prefer to believe Mr. Eldridge. His name means something in the racing world."

"As does Silverthorne," Miss Atwood retorted.

"Perhaps," Camden said with a shrug. "So, what is it to be, Eldridge?"

"This is ridiculous!" Robert cried. "I was here to purchase a horse, and now, somehow, I am the one responsible for the quality of another gentleman's horse?"

"A terrible shame it is, is it not?" Camden flicked something off the shoulder of his coat. "You should have lost that race last year. Bertram, at least, had the good grace to disqualify himself."

Robert drew in a deep breath and steadied his nerves, reigning in the anger he felt. Causing a person to fly into the rafters was another thing Camden enjoyed. "He fell taking a gate and nearly died. I am not sure that is the same as disqualifying himself."

"However, you wish to see it. I will be at the Red Lion when you have come to a decision." He stepped closer to Robert. "I am not a patient man, Eldridge, so do not dawdle." He turned back to James. "I will take Damon with me. I am sure you can afford to stable him at the inn until Mr. Eldridge makes up his mind."

Robert took three deep breaths. There was no choice to be made. Camden had left him with only one option. "I will do it."

"What?" Miss Atwood cried. "You cannot."

"No, I must," he assured her. He could not allow Camden to ban him from every race, nor could he have Camden pursuing him as he did someone who had cheated him. Those fellows rarely survived the encounter.

"I will ride Damon in the next race at Newmarket," he said to Camden, "but he stays at Silverthorne while I am at Mansfield and then accompanies me to my estate when I leave. It is the only way I can prepare him as he needs to be prepared to win a race."

"I will not pay for lodging or feed."

"We will provide all that is needed," James offered. "Is my debt settled?"

Camden nodded. "And it is settled in a more favourable fashion than I had expected, for I lost a good deal on that race last year." He nodded to Robert. "I intend to do better this time." And with that, he called for his own horse and left.

Chapter 7

"We will be in the southern field," Addie told the stable master as she settled into her saddle. She still could not believe that Mr. Eldridge had agreed to Mr. Camden's preposterous offer. If he lost his horse or a thousand pounds to the man, James would feel it his duty to repay such a debt. She would make certain of that since it was his foolishness which led to all of this.

Damon snorted and tossed his head.

"Not yet," she said to him. "We will run when we get to the field. I do not wish for you to use up all your resources in getting there. Mr. Eldridge must know exactly of what you are capable."

Damon snorted and tossed his head again.

"It really does not matter if you agree or not." She patted the side of his neck. How was she going to part with him and not be destroyed by missing him? She blinked at the tears which sprang up in answer to her question. How she wished that there was some horse in their stables who could outrun Damon!

That was it! Maybe there wasn't a horse who could out-run Damon now, but that did not mean there might not be one who, with a little training, could best him. She drew to a stop and turned to the groom who had accompanied her. "Stuart, which horse would you say is next in quality to Damon?"

"Pythias," Stuart replied.

"Can you ride him?" Pythias, a young stallion, was a good choice for a stallion could sire offspring which would make Pythias more valuable than Damon.

"He is a trifle high-spirited, miss, but yes, I have ridden worse."

"Would you please trade your mount for him and bring him to the field?" She needed to see if Pythias had any hope of learning to outrun Damon.

Stuart's brow furrowed for a moment before he assured her that he would do as she asked.

Confident that she had perhaps landed on a solution to her current distress of needing to part with Damon, a flutter of hope lodged in Addie's heart as she rode on to the field alone.

Although it was not the first time she had ridden unat-tended, it was the first time she had felt so alone as she presently did. Mr. Camden had unsettled her and not just a little. She had very much disliked the way the man had found ways to be near her at every turn yesterday. He was not an unattractive gentleman — indeed he was rather handsome — and likely not more than forty or five and forty in age, but he had made her skin crawl more than the thought of being married to her father's friend Mr. North-cott did.

"A bit faster boy." She nudged Damon to a gallop. The mere memory of Mr. Camden's skin-crawling presence made her wish to not be alone for too very long.

"Good morning." Mr. Eldridge had broken away from his group to meet her as she approached. "Why are you alone?"

She scowled. She did not like his scolding tone of voice, even if it was likely because he was as concerned about Mr. Camden and what he might do as she was.

"James has gone to see that the bill at the inn is settled."

"You mean he is gone to see that Camden is gone."

"That is what I said," she retorted.

"I was not criticizing," Mr. Eldridge said with a sidelong look at her as they rode.

She drew and released a deep breath. "I apologize. I should not speak so sharply. I am just a trifle ill-at-ease today."

It was not an excuse. She was anxious. Though her father's condition had not worsened, he had also not made any improvements either. His life hung at the edges of the room as if it could not decide whether to leave or stay. She had begged it to stay, but she knew it would not be for long even if it did grant her wish.

Then, there was the possible presence of Mr. Camden. He owned Damon and could come to Silverthorne at any time to see how his possession fared. She shuddered to think what he might do if he decided that Damon was not progressing as needed or looked anything less than perfect. The world outside her home – the gardens, the stables, the rolling fields, and stands of trees were no longer sanctuaries of peace. Danger lurked within them.

Added to all that, was the knowledge that she would have to part with her horse. It only remained to be seen whether she would have to part with her father or the precious gift he had given her first.

All in all, her nerves were tattered and torn at best.

"At the risk of making you more uneasy..."

She looked at Mr. Eldridge expectantly. He seemed a trifle flustered.

"You cannot ride as you are if we are to train this fellow properly."

"What is wrong with the way I am riding?"

"It is not how he will be ridden in a race. He must grow accustomed to being ridden astride."

"I have no other clothes or saddle, Mr. Eldridge." He could not mean for her to use her current saddle and ride so. It was neither seemly nor safe.

"As always, my sister is prepared for that." He smiled at her and shrugged, perhaps a bit sheepishly. "She is nearly always prepared for any eventuality. It is one of her great talents – as annoying as it might be at times."

"What do you mean, she is prepared?"

"We have brought a saddle from Mansfield and some clothing – breeches, a shirt, and a jacket. Your own footwear will have to suffice. Faith was not sure about the size of your foot."

But she was certain of the size of the rest of her? Addie closed her mouth which had dropped open. She was uncertain as to how she should respond to such a thing. She was not opposed to riding astride, but the thought of wearing breeches while in company and not just on her own was... well... it was not precisely proper. Of course, riding astride in her riding habit would not be all that much more proper. Which brought her to the most pressing problem with the whole scheme.

"Where am I to change?" One did not take off her clothes and put on a new set in the middle of a field, and to ride home and return seemed a foolish waste of time.

"Among the trees over there." He moved his horse a step closer to her as they drew near the group who had accompanied him. "Faith is also wearing breeches as a show of support. She did not wish you to feel too out of place." His tone was gentle and soothing. "It is not the first time she has dressed so."

"Truly?" Addie could not believe that a lady as beautiful

and refined as Miss Eldridge appeared to be would even consider wearing breeches.

"It made it less conspicuous for her to visit the stockbroker."

Addie once again had to close her mouth which had insisted on popping open. A stockbroker?

"Faith," Mr. Eldridge called.

"I believe Miss Atwood could use your assistance in changing her costume while Bertram and I switch Damon's saddle." He had slid from his horse and was standing ready to help Addie dismount from hers.

He was being a trifle demanding, but at present, she did not mind so very much as her brain was not functioning as it should. Her mind was still attempting to wrap itself around her need to change and the fact that Miss Eldridge had visited a stockbroker while dressed in breeches.

Therefore, she allowed him to help her from her horse without a word of protest, which, as it turned out, had been an excellent choice.

Goodness! He was stronger than his lean body suggested. But then, if he worked with horses, he would have to be strong, would he not? She nearly sighed. He could help her from her horse anytime he liked. Standing this close to him was sending a skittering of delight up her spine and warming her from the inside out. She briefly considered climbing back up onto her horse just to have him lift her down again.

"My brother should have mentioned this yesterday."
Miss Eldridge gave her brother a sharp look, and he
stepped away from Addie. "However, I will forgive him
of the oversight, seeing how Mr. Camden had taken him
by surprise and all." She wrapped an arm around Addie's.
"Miss Price is waiting for us. She assures me that she
thinks the clothing will fit, and we have created a screen
with a couple of sheets."

Mr. Eldridge was not wrong. His sister seemed to be
prepared for everything. It was delightful to meet a lady
with such a good mind. It made Addie feel a lot less odd
than she normally did when surrounded by other females
who seemed only capable of discussing stitching and the
weather with an occasional comment about books or
music thrown in to keep things interesting.

"Your brother told me that you visited a stockbroker,"
Addie said as she slipped the breeches up her legs while
still wearing her dress. There might be a screen, but there
was also a breeze causing the bottom of that screen to flutter.

Faith laughed lightly. "I assure you that it was done as
discreetly as possible, but I am fascinated by numbers and
how properly investing one's funds can grow one's worth."

"I can understand that." Addie stood waiting for Susan
to help her unfasten her dress.

"Oh, Addie is very good with numbers," Susan assured
Miss Eldridge.

"I did not wear my stays," Addie whispered as her dress slid to the ground and she stood in her stockings, breeches which fit a bit snugly but not unbearably so, and her chemise. Bending forward to urge Damon to run faster was done more easily when unencumbered by stays.

"I thought you might not have," Faith said with a grin. "I have a short chemise to go under your shirt and then, we must just make certain your jacket is buttoned where it needs to be."

And they did. Addie was cleverly stuffed into the rest of her costume and declared perfect within moments. However, she was not certain how perfect she was. The jacket was not buttoning across her chest as easily as the one Faith wore. She pulled at the front of it, attempting to make the material not pucker.

"I will have to find a bigger size for tomorrow," Miss Eldridge whispered. "My brother likely has one with which he can part – unless, of course, you prefer to bind your breasts. I am not as blessed in that area as you are."

"These are your clothes?" Addie asked in surprise.

Miss Eldridge nodded. "I like to ride unhindered by yards of material at times."

"I used to ride in breeches, but then I turned twelve, and my father would not hear of it."

"My brother would rather that I did not," Miss Eldridge said with a laugh. "However, I can be rather stubborn, and he is more generous with me than he should be."

"He seems very amiable."

"Oh, he is." Miss Eldridge grasped one of Susan's arms and one of Addie's as they exited from behind their screen. "Do not tell him I said so, but while he is friendly to all, that does not mean he is capricious, for he is also a most loyal friend."

"Why should we not tell him?" Susan asked before Addie could.

"I do not wish for the praise to go to his head," Miss Eldridge replied, "especially since I am not finished scolding him for leaving Mr. Bertram when he was injured. Therefore, if I were to say he is a great friend while at the same time accusing him of deserting his friend, well, that just would not do."

Addie chuckled. "Have you always had such a good relationship?"

"Oh, we argue constantly," Miss Eldridge replied.

"But not to the point of injury," Susan replied. "He cares a great deal for you."

"And I for him, but he needs to be pushed at times. My mother made me promise to see him well-settled so that he would not idle away either his time or his estate. He has made great strides in improving himself, which is why I wish to be able to continue to remind him of his failure as needed." She lowered her voice. "Never to his harm as you said, Susan, but just to remind him of his desire to improve."

That seemed a reasonable thing to Addie. She would likely remind James of their current situation in the future to keep him from finding himself in such a precarious position as he now did. It would be irresponsible really to do otherwise, would it not?

"Now," Miss Eldridge continued with a chuckle, "shall we see if my brother can remember how to train a horse when presented with you in breeches. He was rather taken with you the first time he saw you ride, and you are looking quite delectable."

"Oh, that will not do!" Addie's cheeks burned. "This is too improper. We have only two weeks to do what needs to be done. I can ride astride in a dress."

"No," Miss Eldridge protested, "the material will get in the way. I should not have teased."

"What do you think, Susan? Do I do as Miss Eldridge says or put my dress back on?"

Susan did not even take a moment to think before answering. "You cannot. You must do what is best for Mr. Eldridge. He cannot lose his horse."

Leave it to Susan to bring things back into focus. They were attempting to save Mr. Eldridge's horse or his thousand pounds. She needed to remember that.

"Please, call me Faith," Miss Eldridge said to both Susan and Addie.

Addie looked down at her attire. Whatever discomfort she felt must come second to what needs to be done for

Mr. Eldridge, but... "Are you certain?" she asked Susan, who nodded.

"Is her horse ready?" Faith called to Tom and Mr. Eldridge.

"Ye—" Mr. Eldridge did not form the full word as he turned and saw Addie.

"As I said, you look perfect," Faith whispered.

"Then, help her up," she commanded her brother, who did as instructed with only a few stumbles while Tom looked excessively amused.

Addie sat atop her horse and waited for Mr. Eldridge to mount his.

"Oh!" she cried upon seeing Stuart approaching on Pythias. "I nearly forgot in all the changes that needed to be made."

Tom, Faith, Susan, and Mr. Eldridge turned toward her.

She smiled. "Damon might not be Silverthorne's best." She waved her hand in Stuart's direction. "Meet Pythias."

Chapter 8

His mind had turned to gruel. It must have. Miss Atwood's charms had stolen his senses. That was the only thing it could be, for surely, she was not telling him that he had convinced Camden to take the wrong horse. He turned to mount his horse.

"What do you mean Damon might not be the best?" Tom asked.

So, Robert had not misheard Miss Atwood.

"Camden will not be pleased to be taken for a fool," Tom continued.

"He has not been," Miss Atwood replied.

"If you told him that Damon was the best and then there is another which is better, how could he not come to that conclusion?" Tom questioned.

Robert nodded. His mind would have formed those very words had it been at liberty to form any words at all. Did she have to look so enticing in her breeches and jacket? He had known it was a possibility – Tom had warned him it was — but he had not been prepared for the reality of just how alluring she would be.

Miss Atwood tipped her head and huffed as one eyebrow rose. "If you would allow me to continue."

Tom waved his hand for her to proceed.

"Stuart."

"Yes, miss." Stuart looked uneasily between his mistress and Tom.

"In your opinion which horse is the next in quality to Damon?"

"Pythias, miss," the groom answered. "As I told you."

Miss Atwood smiled at him. "I have not forgotten. I just needed Mr. Bertram to hear it."

The groom gave a nod and cast a sidelong look in Tom's direction.

"Can you tell Mr. Bertram why Pythias was not among the horses shown to Mr. Camden yesterday?"

"You said he was not ready, miss."

"And why was he not ready?"

"He's only just learned to accept a saddle and rider."

Addie nodded and, after a word of thanks to Stuart, turned to Tom. "Pythias is a stallion, not a gelding. Therefore, he would be of far greater value to Mr. Camden than Damon. If Pythias can win a race or two, his worth as a sire would be great."

"Does that not make our position even more precarious?" Faith asked.

Miss Atwood shook her head. "No, it puts us in a more favourable light."

"How?" Robert finally managed to get a word from his brain to his mouth.

"Well, Mr. Eldridge, while training Damon against your horse, as well as some from Silverthorne's stables, it was discovered that Pythias shows great promise. Until this time, he has been untried, but as soon as we recognized his potential, we thought it our duty to inform Mr. Camden of our discovery should he wish to alter his former decision. After all, as I understood it, Mr. Camden was somewhat disappointed that Damon was a gelding. However, should he not wish to take Pythias in Damon's stead, he must know that a formidable challenger will be added to the race under Silverthorne's name."

Robert shook his head. "He'll not allow you to race against him."

She opened her mouth to protest.

"You heard what he said to me," Robert added. "And you know why I am training Damon."

"Because you do not wish to part with your horse." She skewered him with a pointed look. "Which, as you might imagine, I can understand."

Her words hit their mark. He couldn't just dismiss her plan and her hopes to retain Damon out of hand. "What do you think, Bertram?"

Tom shrugged. "Camden is a slippery fellow. He'll likely find a way to end up with Damon, Pythias, and Hugo."

"But he only gets Hugo if Mr. Eldridge and Damon do not win," Miss Atwood inserted.

"We will win," Robert assured her.

"Not if Pythias proves as good as he might be."

"We should consult James," Miss Price inserted with a timid smile for her friend.

Miss Atwood's eyes narrowed. "It is a good plan."

"I did not say it was not," Miss Price countered.

"Shall we test Pythias?" Robert asked before anything further could be said. Had Miss Atwood not told him earlier that she was on edge? There was no point in arguing the validity of this scheme at present, especially when he had no idea just how good the young stallion Pythias was.

Miss Atwood nodded silently, and Robert maneuvered Hugo a step closer to her.

"If we can save your horse, we will," he whispered. "But give us time to consider it."

Her lips trembled, and she pressed them together.

"Are you confident enough to run Pythias against us?" Robert asked Stuart. "If not, we can change horses."

"I think I can do it," Stuart replied.

"Pull up if you feel he is going to cause issues."

"Yes, sir."

He looked at Miss Atwood, lovely Miss Atwood, resplendent in her blue jacket as she sat atop her horse and valiantly overcoming her emotions, and tipped his head. "Are you ready?"

She nodded.

"Standing is allowed and encouraged in this race." The comment brought a smile to her lips as it was meant to do.

"No wager this time?" she asked.

He shook his head. "I must keep an eye on how your horse is running." He moved to take his place in line next to where Stuart was. "I wish to know his movements before I ride him."

"Make sure you are watching her horse," Tom whispered before cuffing his shoulder.

As much as he wished to tell his friend that that would not be an issue, he could not, for Robert knew that keeping his attention on the horse Miss Atwood was riding and not Miss Atwood was going to pose a struggle.

However, to his surprise, he did not find it to be as great a struggle to keep his eyes off Miss Atwood as expected. Instead, his attention was arrested by something else entirely. Pythias was good, excessively good.

When the race was over, he circled Pythias, eyeing him carefully. He was a beauty. "It would be a risk," he muttered. "A definite gamble," he added with a shake of his head.

If it were him, he would keep this fellow under wraps for another year and then race him. The proceeds from his offspring would be good. However, this was not his horse.

It was Silverthorne's, and there were inducements that money could not buy which pushed him to consider Miss Atwood's plan. He knew that some horses – well, most to him – were more than commodities, more than a simple means of transportation, and more than a source of entertainment and a game of chance on a racecourse. They were trusted companions, and Miss Atwood was being forced to part with such a creature. This plan could possibly save her such heartache.

He looked her direction to discover she was watching him closely.

"You may be correct, Miss Atwood. Pythias is indeed a fine horse."

Her smile reached from her lips to her eyes.

"However, it is too early to tell how good he is," he cautioned. "It could be a stroke of luck. He might not be able to run in a group. His jumping might not be right." Robert rubbed the back of his neck. "However, I think we should, at least, speak to your brother and consider the possibility. I should very much hate for Camden to discover you had a faster horse in your possession when he made the deal with your brother for Damon." Especially since, it would be his neck, and not that of James Atwood, which would be at risk, for Camden had already warned Robert about appearing to be a cheat where choosing the best horse was concerned.

With that settled, they returned to exercising their animals. Two more races added proof to the potential contained in Pythias as he won one and came a close second in the other. Even if he were running Hugo at full speed instead of attempting to stay behind to watch the other horses — and Miss Atwood — Robert was not entirely certain he could successfully hold off the young stallion.

Finally, just before he was going to call their session over, Robert took Miss Atwood's place on her horse, while she sat on his to watch the race. He did not wish to have her attempt to race on an unfamiliar horse. He had done it many times, but he doubted she had.

"I will ride Pythias tomorrow." He patted Damon's neck. "Today is your day to show me what you can do." He leaned forward. "Take to the sky," he whispered as he winked at Miss Atwood who smiled.

Damon snorted and was off. Hooves pounded the ground at a furious pace even after having run as much as Damon had. Robert shifted his weight from the saddle and fully into his toes. He pumped the reins against Damon's neck, urging him onward. This was a horse who delighted in running and who could most certainly be a champion. They rounded the end of the course, which was marked by Tom and Faith, and returned to where Miss Atwood and Miss Price waited.

"I should have agreed to giving Camden a thousand pounds," Robert said as he drew close to Miss Atwood after allowing Damon a time to walk. "He is good for it."

"I told you he was the best," Miss Atwood teased.

"Well, Hugo did beat him."

"Once."

Robert laughed. "Yes, well, I suppose we will have to hope it was only once and that Damon can be the victor on the day when it is necessary."

"Hope?" she asked in a teasing tone, though her eyes contained sadness. "Can you not guarantee it, Mr. Eldridge?"

"I wish I could," he answered honestly as he swung down from Damon.

He could get used to helping Miss Atwood from Hugo. He held her waist after her feet were on the ground instead of releasing it. "I wish I could make this all go away," he whispered.

"As do I," she admitted softly.

One at a time, he peeled his fingers away from her, willing himself to release her rather than pull her to him.

"Do you wish to change your costume here?" he asked.

She shook her head. "I have wished to ride astride for these past seven years. I should like to take full advantage of the necessity. I will just gather my things, and Stuart can see to the extra saddle." She started toward the trees where she had changed. "You will return to Silverthorne with me, will you not? I should enjoy a bit of company."

"Whatever you wish," Robert assured her.

Whatever she wished? Yes, that was exactly what he

wanted to do for her. Could one lose his heart to a female he had only just met, or was it the way those breeches embraced her figure which was addling his thinking? No, it was likely not that, for he had felt the same when she was wearing a dress. However, it could still just be her beauty calling to him. Or, he thought as he turned away from watching her and toward Tom, who had joined him while Faith went with Miss Atwood and Miss Price to disassemble the dressing room in the trees, it could be her love for horses which drew him to her like a moth to a flame.

"You have a good chance of winning," Tom said.

"Did you doubt I would?"

"No. I know your skill. How many times have I lost to you?"

"Nearly every time."

Tom nodded. "You have a skill with horses that most do not." He drew and released a breath. "Addie seems to share that whatever it is with you." He shook his head. "It would be a sight to behold the quality of stables you and she could create."

Robert turned and looked toward the trees where the ladies were. He had to admit Tom was right. Miss Atwood was special. She knew horses better than any lady he had met, and he had met several who claimed to know horses. Of course, at least one of those ladies had been attempting to seduce him. However, marriage should likely be about more than the way a lady looked in a pair of breeches and how well she sat on a horse, right?

Tom nudged Robert's shoulder with his own. "Faith approves of her."

Robert chuckled. "Is that your true purpose in speaking to me?"

"No, your sister did not direct me to tell you that. I thought you might wish to know." He shrugged. "And for what it is worth, I think you would suit."

Robert pulled in a deep breath and released it. "I think we would, too," he admitted. "And I am almost entirely certain it is not the fit of her breeches or the cut of her jacket making me think so."

Chapter 9

For a week after that first day on which Addie had presented her idea to save Damon, she, James, and Mr. Eldridge met to race their mounts against one another. For the same week, Mr. Eldridge rode either Damon or Pythias while Addie rode Hugo and James rode whichever of Silverthorne's horses Mr. Eldridge was not riding. For that same week, the three of them would afterwards return to Silverthorne Hall and have tea. And, for that same week, Addie slept more in the chair in her father's room than in her bed.

However, one week and a day after that first day on which Addie had presented her idea to save Damon, she did not venture from her house. The horses remained in the stable. The chair beside her father's bed was taken away, and she no longer had to wonder whether she would have to give up her father or Damon first, for she knew the answer.

Within three days of her father's passing, all that needed to be done in seeing him quietly laid to rest in the churchyard next to his wife and parents had been done, and while the churchyard grew just that much more crowded, Silverthorne Hall was left with a gaping hole.

However, it was not just the house which seemed incomplete, so did Addie's heart.

"Are you going to come with me?" James asked five days after their family had shrunken by one. "I cannot ride two horses at once."

"Take Stuart. He is an excellent rider." She barely glanced up from the toast she was breaking into pieces on her plate rather than eating. It was better if all the heartbreak was done with at once. She simply could not bear to ride Damon knowing that tomorrow, he would leave with Mr. Eldridge and likely never return.

Addie was uncertain which was most painful, to know that Damon would be gone forever, or that Mr. Eldridge would be. It was likely both. She had come to view Mr. Eldridge as a very good friend, much as she did Damon. They both seemed to understand her and wish for her to be as she was and not as society demanded her to be. Neither cared how much she loved horses or the interest she took in understanding the workings of an estate and stable.

Such acceptance reminded her of her father and was what was missing and had made her brother such a ninny after he had left for school. When he had come home at that first holiday, he no longer viewed her as he always had. He saw her through the eyes of his friends, and they viewed her as no different than any other female of their acquaintance.

"Adela, please." James sat down next to her and stopped her hands. "You cannot waste away in the house. Think of how distressed Father would be to see it."

She clenched her teeth together and swallowed the immediate sorrow which rose at the mention of her father. Shaking her head, she whispered, "I cannot. I simply cannot."

How did one abide so much loss all at once?

James released her hands and rose. "Then, I am going to find Camden and tell him that Pythias is the better horse."

Her head snapped up. "No, you cannot! What will he do to you? How shall I live if you are not here?"

"You got on well without me before." He shrugged and brushed at his sleeve.

"I had Father!" She paused to contain her emotions. "And Damon. Now, I have neither." The tears would not remain contained any longer.

"I shall never forgive myself," her brother muttered. "Not in a thousand years. I deserve whatever Camden does to me."

Before he could get more than two steps closer to the door, she had him in her arms. "Do not leave me. I would trade a thousand horses for you." She sniffled and attempted to smile. "Even if you are a monstrous fool."

"Then come with me," he begged. "It is not like you to allow life to happen without your approval. You have not eaten a proper meal in nearly a week, and you do not sleep as you should. I fear for your health. At least, come out and see the sun."

She squeezed him tighter. This was the brother she remembered from her childhood – the one who teased and taunted her but would have run through a cold winter night with only his nightshirt and slippers to keep him warm if she had required such to see her safe and happy. This was the brother who had vanished four years ago and been replaced with the one who rarely gave her a second glance on his way to do whatever it was which caught his fancy.

"I have missed you," she whispered.

"I have missed me, too," he answered before giving her hair a kiss. "Now, change your clothes. We are going riding."

"Wait," he called before she could exit the room. "Eat this." He snatched what was left of her piece of toast off her plate and thrust it at her.

She thanked him and resumed scurrying up to her room to don her breeches and a green jacket which fit much better than the blue one Faith had given her at first. She sighed as she slipped her arms into its sleeves. The fabric of the coat wrapped her in its comfort, and the familiar scent of horses and fresh air, mingled with a hint of cedar, brought to mind images of the coat's former owner for that was precisely how he smelled whenever he lifted her down from her horse.

Several minutes later, though not long enough to have her hair as neatly coiffured as her maid would have liked, Addie joined her brother, who shoved another piece of almost warm toast at her along with a piece of lovely stinky cheese, and together they made their way to the stables.

"I was beginning to wonder if I should come find you," Mr. Eldridge said in greeting to James. "Miss Atwood, I am happy to see you."

And he looked it. His lips were curled into a smile wide enough to give a bit of plumpness to his cheeks, and his eyes shone with delight. She had not realized until this moment, as she stood in front of him while he smiled at her and she desperately attempted to swallow her dry toast quickly enough to give a proper greeting, just how much she had missed him. Seeing him somehow made her world seem a little less barren. She pushed the unwelcome thought of his eminent departure from her mind.

"It was a lonely few days riding without you," he admitted as he helped her mount his horse. "I believe even Hugo missed you, did you not, boy?" He stroked the beast's nose as he asked it. Hugo tossed his head as if nodding yes, and Addie did something she did not think she would ever do again, she laughed.

This was where she longed to be. This was where things

were perfect in the world, even when they were not. Here, with Mr. Eldridge.

"That is a wonderful sound," James said. "But then, I knew if there was anything which could rouse your spirits it would be a horse." He winked at her and then clucked to Pythias.

While her brother was right about horses being excellent at lifting her out of a blue mood, it was the gentleman swinging up onto the back of Damon who was truly responsible for the smile she not only wore but felt. Her smile faltered as the unwelcome thought she had pushed away before refused to remain tucked away. Tomorrow, her world would once again turn bleak for Mr. Eldridge would be gone.

"Are you well?" Mr. Eldridge drew alongside her.

She nodded.

"Truly?" He did not sound as if he believed her.

"As well as can be expected."

"Allow me to extend my condolences once again," Mr. Eldridge said.

"Thank you, but it is not just that."

"It is not?"

She shook her head. "You are leaving tomorrow."

"Ah, and so is Damon." He nodded. "I understand."

She shook her head once again. "*You* are leaving tomorrow," she repeated, adding emphasis to the you. "I will miss more than just Damon."

"You will?"

"James is only capable of being mildly entertaining." She should just admit to loving Mr. Eldridge, but she had not felt so nervous about anything since climbing back onto a horse after having lost her seat when she was twelve. What if he did not feel about her as she did him? She was not certain her heart could withstand such a disappointment.

"And what of Miss Price and Faith? My sister is remaining at Mansfield for a time. If Tom's father continues to strengthen, then she will join me for the races when Tom does. However, if Sir Thomas should decline, then, I will return once the races are done."

He looked at her expectantly, and, if she was not mistaken, a bit hopefully. The expression gave her the confidence to push forward.

"Life is not very long, is it?"

He blinked. "No, it is not."

"I had not realized just how short it was until I became an orphan." Her lips quirked upward. It seemed odd to call someone as old as she was an orphan. It was not as if she was without care. She was just without parents.

"I can appreciate that since I am also an orphan."

"One should not be too slow in acting on that which one wishes to do." Her heart beat wildly behind her ribs. She could not allow him to leave without making her desires known.

He tilted his head as he studied her with a look of concern.

"I have not lost my senses," she assured him. "I am just struck by the brevity of time to accomplish what one wishes to accomplish is all. Did you not feel the same when you came into your inheritance?"

He shook his head. "I was too terrified to consider that at the time."

He was terrified? It was dashed hard to believe. He had always appeared so confident to her.

"I was a bit like James," he explained. "I spent more time indulging my desires than preparing for my future." He smiled sheepishly at her. "Thankfully, like James, I have a sister with a great deal of sense. She did not allow me to hide from my new-found responsibilities. I think I was struck more by the fact that life is not just a lark than I was the brevity of life when my father died, and my frivolous nature was drawn along to become a trifle more sober."

"And my more sober nature is feeling it should perhaps be more frivolous – but not rash," she added. Rashness was never wise. Even seemingly spontaneous decisions must be given some consideration before they are made – such as the one she had just made to share her admiration with him.

"To answer your question more directly," she continued, "while I love Miss Price dearly, for one could not find a better friend, and I very much enjoy spending time with Miss Eldridge, neither of them is you."

"Come with me." His request was immediate and eager as if he had just been waiting to be given permission to make it.

Go with him? To his estate? It was a shocking idea, and yet it also felt as if it was perfectly natural.

"Please. Come with me," he implored.

"Alone?" She needed to think this through. She could not just blurt a yes as she wished to do, for she could not stay with him at his home alone and retain any sort of good reputation.

"No, no, of course not. I meant with your brother, though I will admit that your brother will be little more than a chaperone." He smiled. "A chaperone who can ride quite well – well enough to enter a race."

Right. The race. For her plan to work, her brother would need to be at the race to offer Pythias to Mr. Camden. "That would be best, I suppose. It would seem odd for you to show up with two of our horses for Mr. Camden."

"Yes, there is that," Mr. Eldridge agreed. "But I was truly only asking so that I might not have to be separated from you."

Surprisingly, a heart that had just suffered great grief and was expecting further sorrow was not incapable of being excessively happy. He liked her so much, then? She had realized when they had been riding each day before her father died that even when his sister and Susan were with them, he had paid her marked attention, and she had hoped he might admire her as much as she admired him.

"I should like to discover if we might suit." He glanced to where her brother was just ahead of him. "I know your father has just died, and to ask to court you or anything else is not proper, but..." He shrugged. "Life is short."

"Indeed, it is," she agreed. "I will see what James says." He would say yes. She would make certain of it.

"Then, perhaps we should catch up to him."

"No, he can wait." She was in no hurry to have her brother intrude upon the wonderful way she was feeling at this moment. Mr. Eldridge liked her – enough to wish to court her. "I wish Father had gotten to meet you." Her thoughts would not stay contained in her mind. She felt compelled by some unseen force to share them with him.

"I would have liked that. From seeing his stables, I would have to say that I think he and I would have had a great number of things about which to converse. Was he always good with horses?"

"As far back as I can remember." Her father had been a bit like Mr. Eldridge. He was fabulously good at getting a horse to do just what he wanted the creature to do. And to see him ride. She sighed. He would fly along the field as if he and his mount were one. Her desire to be like him was why she rode as she did whenever she could – fast as the clouds before a mighty north wind, that was how her father had described it.

In front of her, James rose from his saddle, leaning forward, and urging Pythias onward – up one incline, down another, around a stone tower that he had built just for the purpose of having a place to turn, and then back towards them before repeating the circuit.

"He is not half bad," she muttered.

Mr. Eldridge chuckled. "No, he is not. There is a great deal of potential both in Pythias and your brother."

"Do you truly believe so?" When she turned to look at him, she expected to see him near her, but not so very close that his leg was brushing hers.

"I'd like to collect on the race I won."

His gaze slipped from her eyes to her lips and then returned. She swallowed.

"A kiss?"

He nodded. "And your promise to go home with me when your brother does."

Heat spread across her cheeks. "You did win it," she acquiesced as she leaned towards him, meeting him halfway on his quest for her lips.

Thundering across a field on the back of a great racer was nothing compared to the exhilaration she felt when his lips met hers. She clutched Hugo's reins tightly in one hand as her other hand, of its own accord, found its way to Mr. Eldridge's jaw. A small groan escaped him as she stroked his smooth, well-shaven skin. His mouth claimed hers more greedily, his tongue teased her lips, sending shivers through her.

Then, just as her lips opened and her tongue touched his, he pulled away.

"That was likely not a good idea," he whispered. His hand cupped her cheek. His thumb stroked her lips. "For I would very much like to do that again and again."

He was not alone in such a desire. "Then –" She paused. Her voice sounded shockingly breathy and wanton! "Then," she began again in a slightly less aroused tone, "I suggest you continue to win races, and I will give you one kiss per win."

He chuckled. "If that is the reward, I shan't ever lose another race."

"You might," Addie said as she clucked to Hugo and pressed her heels into his side.

"And what will you claim if you win," Mr. Eldridge called after her.

Addie shrugged. "I have no idea." And it was the truth, for she could not think of a thing in the world that Mr. Eldridge could provide which she wanted more at this moment than another kiss.

Chapter 10

Later as Robert sat watching Miss Atwood put Hugo through his paces, he broached his idea to take her home with him to her brother. There was no part of him that wanted to be parted from her for any length of time. "It might be beneficial if your sister were to join us at Stonegate. She is excellent with Hugo."

"I would like very much to have Addie join us. I would rather not leave her alone just now."

That was precisely the answer for which Robert had been hoping.

"Are you asking so that she can continue to help train Hugo, or is it more?" James gave Robert a pointed look.

"More." Robert held James's gaze.

"She has just lost her father."

"Yes, I know."

"She is vulnerable."

"I am not exploiting the circumstances. I would have asked your father should he have survived for me to do so."

"It would be an advantage to have Silverthorne so closely tied to you."

Was that an accusation he heard in young Atwood's voice?

"I will not deny that such is true," Robert replied, "but that is not why I wish to see if your sister and I would suit."

James waited silently for Robert to continue.

"Actually, I am quite certain we would suit. She is unique. Part of that is how well she is acquainted with horses, but there is something more. It will almost certainly sound foolish to you, but whatever it is which draws me to her is indescribable." He blew out a breath. "She fits. It is as if she was designed to be part of my life."

"Is it as if you can see her sitting beside the hearth with you on a winter's evening?" James's eyes were no longer fixed on Robert but had shifted to look off into the distance.

"That is it precisely." It was curious that James should understand such a thing, for up until now, Robert had not thought he was the sort to think as deeply as something such as that would take. "You speak as if you are acquainted with the feeling."

James nodded. "There is a lady who has been particularly difficult to not continually think of in such a fashion."

That was intriguing. "Is there a reason why you should rid your mind of this particular young woman?"

"I am in no way ready to take on a wife. You know the mess I have made of things."

That was undeniable. James Atwood had made a grand mess of things. However, just because one made poor choices did not mean one must always be doomed to be less than wise. "I nearly allowed Tom to die. I guarantee you that I will not make the same mistake again, and I assume you will not engage in a game of chance with the likes of Camden ever again."

James's head bobbed up and down slowly as if he was both agreeing and pondering the thought. "I am still not ready. Silverthorne will need a mistress but not until the master has found his footing." He shrugged. "I had hoped to have Addie to help me with the transition, but I can see how she watches you."

She watched him? That was a pleasant thought. Very pleasant, indeed.

"You would treat her well," James continued. "You did not have to help us when you heard about Camden, but you did. Your character seems sound, and," his lips tipped upwards, "you would not keep my sister from the one thing which soothes her soul."

"Horses?"

James nodded.

"We are alike in that way," Robert admitted. "She seems a natural with them."

"She always has been. I believe she inherited that from

our father." There was a wistfulness to Atwood's tone. It seemed his confidence might need some bolstering.

"Then, he has passed it on to both his children."

James shook his head.

"I am not flattering you," Robert said. "Horses are a serious business to me. I do not compliment where it is not due. I will allow that there might be more of a natural bent in Miss Atwood, but I believe you have the potential to be nearly as good as your sister."

That sister was just rounding the stone pillar and racing toward the makeshift gate they had erected to allow the horses to practice their gait coming into a jump. Without taking his eyes off Miss Atwood, Robert continued his conversation with James.

"You will need to become every bit as good as her if you wish for Silverthorne to succeed and provide for you and your family. Whatever you do, do not hide from the responsibility. It will not go away and spending what you do not have to spend will not add to your coffers. One day, I hope to be as good at managing accounts as my sister is."

James chuckled. "Where would we men be without sisters such as ours?"

"I would rather not speculate on such a disaster," Robert replied with a laugh. "It is a good thing someone in our families was born with the sense to remain focused on what was truly important."

"Indeed, it is," James agreed.

"I have agreed to take you with me when I go to Stonegate," he called to his sister as she approached.

The smile which lit Miss Atwood's face was the stuff for which a gentleman wished, or, at least, it was for Robert. To know that she was so happy to not be separated from him was delightful beyond compare.

"You will be joining us for tea, will you not, Eldridge?" James asked.

"You could not keep me from it."

James shook his head. "Insufferable, that is what a gent becomes once his heart is engaged. The same happened to my friend Willet."

"I beg your pardon?" Addie asked in surprise. "Mr. Willet has found a lady?"

"He thinks he has. Her father is not so certain of the fact, however."

"That I can understand," Addie muttered.

"What do you mean?" James questioned.

"Mr. Willet is charming to be sure, but how shall I say this?"

"Directly, I would guess," James muttered.

"That is often the best way to say things," Robert inserted. "Or so my sister says."

"I do like your sister." Miss Atwood laughed.

"Tell me what is wrong with my charming friend which would cause a father to not readily give his daughter to the chap?" James asked.

"Unless Mr. Willet has changed since the last time I saw him, he seems the sort to pose a danger to a lady's virtue, and as such, I would be reticent to tie my daughter to him."

That was rather direct, Robert thought. Much like his sister would have said something.

"If a gentleman has wandered before he is married," she continued, "he might also wander after he is married. There is often no acknowledgment of the sanctity of the marriage agreement present in such gentlemen. Just consider Mr. Crawford."

"He was not married," Robert inserted. "Indeed, he is not married now, though he soon will be."

Miss Atwood arched an eyebrow. "*He* was not married, but Mrs. Rushworth was. And, Mr. Crawford was not entirely free, for he had made an offer to Fanny! None of those things kept him from doing what he did." She shrugged. "Mr. Willet reminds me of Mr. Crawford. Both are very capable of charming whatever they want from whomever they wish to take it. Unless, of course, it is a lady of good sense such as Fanny is."

Miss Atwood's ability to draw from one disaster and project it as a possibility on another situation was also a great deal like what Faith would do, and Faith was most often right in her insights. "Henry Crawford is not that way any longer," Robert assured Miss Atwood.

"I am happy to hear it, but there is no assurance that Mr. Willet has changed."

"Have you always felt this way about my friend?" James asked in surprise.

His sister nodded.

"And you did not tell me?"

She shook her head. "You would not have listened, for he had charmed you. I dare say he was with you when you wagered against Mr. Camden."

From the expression James wore, his sister's assumption was dead accurate.

"He tried to charm me once," Miss Atwood added.

"He did what?" James cried in surprise.

"He tried to charm me. It was after I had come back from riding, and he met me in the stables."

"And you never told me?" There was a growl of displeasure in James's tone as there should be. Robert would have been just as angered to hear such a thing from his sister.

She shook her head. "You would not have listened. You were not yourself for some time."

"For how long have I not been myself?"

James was looking horrified with all that was being revealed, and Robert felt sorry for the fellow. Facing one's shortcomings was not something which was done easily. The reality of having failed miserably was the sort of thing that could send a man staggering backward with its weight. He knew. He had felt it.

"Since the day before you went to school until," she shrugged, "this morning."

James sat open-mouthed for a moment before asking, "I was so terrible that you could not tell me about a friend who tried to seduce you?"

"You wagered away my horse."

Oh, that had to have hurt. Robert kept his eyes forward and rode silently, attempting not to make even a small interference between brother and sister.

James blew out a great breath. "I see your point, and I cannot apologize enough."

"I know," Miss Atwood said softly.

The two Atwoods joined Robert in riding in silence for a time.

That Robert had been allowed to be a part of such a discussion between sister and brother was no small thing. He knew how often, when broached in company, things which were of a delicate nature were met with a look which said "Not here. Not now." Therefore, to be allowed to be privy to the conversation Miss Atwood and her brother had just had, proved to him more than words ever could that he was indeed thought of as a very close friend.

"Were we expecting callers?" Miss Atwood asked her brother as they came up to the stables.

A fine coach could just be seen standing on the drive before the house.

"No, we were not," James replied. "Shall we ride to the house and send the horses to the stables from there?"

It was agreed that such a plan was best, and after a

groom had been informed, the three of them proceeded to the house.

A well-dressed lady in a sophisticated looking red carriage dress was just being helped from her carriage as Robert swung down from his horse.

"Aunt Edith?" James approached the lady who was now standing in front of the house. "I did not know to expect you."

"Did your father not tell you that I was arriving?"

"Father died," Miss Atwood said.

Aunt Edith looked from one Atwood sibling to another. "Died? That cannot be."

"It has not yet been a week since he left us," James explained. "A letter was sent."

"I was not at home." Aunt Edith was not looking well.

"Come inside." Miss Atwood took her aunt by the arm and helped her up the steps to the door. "We were just about to have tea."

"I was at a friend's estate, discussing the particulars of a gently bred young lady's introduction to society. I knew he was not well when he wrote to me regarding you, Adela, but he is truly gone?"

"Yes, Aunt, he is."

"My brother is gone?"

"I am sorry to say he is," James answered.

"Oh, well, that is a shock, is it not?" Aunt Edith took a seat in the chair to which she had been led. "Quite a shock." She pulled a handkerchief from her reticule and dabbed at her eyes.

"Are you well?" Robert barely caught the soft whisper between niece and aunt.

"I am uncertain, but it does make my arrival timely."

"How so?" James settled into a chair near his aunt.

"I am here to collect Adela as your father requested."

"Collect me?"

Apparently, Miss Atwood had no idea she was in need of collecting.

"Yes, your father wished for you to have a season, and so he thought it best if I were to introduce you at a few house parties this summer and then make certain you are prepared for your debut next season. I would take you to town now, but the season is half over and there is so much I do not know about your training."

The lady continued to dab at her eyes while attempting to not appear affected by the news of her brother's death. She must be one of those who frowned upon displays of emotion.

"I cannot go with you."

"It is not a matter of if you can, my dear. You are to go with me. I have it in a letter from Mr. Fulton with your father's signature. The monies necessary for your dresses and such have already been transferred to my husband's account. He would have journeyed with me, but I was going to visit Blanche, you see."

Robert shifted on the couch where he sat.

"Aunt Edith," James Atwood said, "this is Mr. Eldridge. Mr. Eldridge, this is my aunt Mrs. Edith Bellingham. She was my father's sister."

"Mr. Eldridge?" Aunt Edith looked at him skeptically. "I have not heard of you before."

"Mr. Eldridge is a recent addition to our circle of intimates," James replied.

"Indeed? He must be very well acquainted with you if you allow your sister to dress as she is in his presence." There was no mistaking the censure in Mrs. Bellingham's tone.

"Father would not have an issue with how Addie is dressed for training a horse," James said.

"Yes, well, your father knew how I felt about what he allowed your sister to do."

So, it seemed Mrs. Bellingham was not the sort to keep her displeasure to herself.

"And we are very well acquainted." Miss Atwood's cheeks were a brilliant red, and she pulled at the sleeves of her jacket. "Are we not, Robert?"

Robert attempted to keep his expression from showing his surprise and pleasure at hearing her use his Christian name. "Yes, very well acquainted."

He could not quite read Miss Atwood's expression, but there seemed to be some desperation in it.

"It is not to be made known abroad," she said with a

small smile for him. "What with Father falling ill and then..." She paused. Her throat moved up and down. No doubt she was attempting to contain her emotions. "And then, with Father's death, things could not be announced as they should have been."

"I am not certain I follow," Mrs. Bellingham said.

Robert was in agreement about that. He also was not certain he understood what Miss Atwood was attempting to say.

"I do not need to be presented to society."

Miss Atwood sent him another look of desperation. If only he could piece the puzzle together to help her.

"Of course, you do my dear," her aunt protested. "After a time of mourning, as is proper, you must find a husband."

"I have no need to find a husband."

"Do not be foolish, child. We all need husbands. James is not going to house you forever."

"He does not have to." Miss Atwood looked directly at Robert, her eyes pleading with him to help her.

Oh! Now, he understood what she was trying to imply. Or, at least, he hoped he did, for he was willing to give her whatever assistance she needed, even to the extent he thought she was implying.

"You cannot live on your own. It is unseemly." Mrs. Bellingham's brows rose. "However, seeing how you are currently dressed and knowing how your father allowed you to behave makes me wonder if you know what unseemly is."

There was that distinct note of censure in the woman's voice again.

"She will not be living on her own," Robert inserted. "She will be my wife." He held Miss Atwood's gaze as he made the announcement. Thankfully, it appeared he had understood her, and his declaration was met with a pleased smile.

He was betrothed. Wouldn't that come as a surprise to his sister and Tom? It would likely be nearly as much of a surprise to them as it was to him. However, since they had both suggested to him that he should consider Miss Atwood, he had no doubt as to their joy at such news. In fact, he suspected that they would be as delighted by this startling development as he was.

Chapter 11

Did she dare to nod her assurance to her startled brother while her aunt sought for words? Addie thought not. It would not do for Aunt Edith to think there was anything which smacked of scheming taking place. Aunt Edith had no tolerance whatsoever for scheming. Indeed, she had little tolerance for anything that might involve enjoyment, for to Aunt Edith, duty and responsibility were paramount to anything else. Proper decorum and an appearance that all was well – even when it most certainly was not – were prized.

How could a sister, who claimed in properly understated terms to love her brother, hear the news of that brother's death and not faint dead away and dissolve into a puddle of tears? To Addie, Aunt Edith's always calm and controlled demeanor was not natural. Not that Aunt Edith was always calm.

No, when Aunt Edith was displeased, she struggled, much as she was doing right now, to keep her features and her tongue in good regulation.

These were not the only flaws her aunt possessed, however. There was one more fault which could be laid at Aunt Edith's feet, and, in the world in which Addie lived, it was perhaps the greatest fault of all. To Aunt Edith, stables were the domain of grooms and coachmen. It was acceptable for a gentleman to oversee the work of his servants – Addie's grandfather always had, which necessitated, in Aunt Edith's way of thinking, that such an activity was acceptable – but a gentleman must not take it upon himself to muck out a stall or rub down his mount for those activities were, in Aunt Edith's opinion, beneath him. Addie had heard her father argue about that very thing with his sister on more than one occasion. It was perhaps why Aunt Edith was not invited to visit very often, for each visit would, almost certainly, include some sort of remonstration to her brother about how things ought to be done.

Had her father been in his right mind when he sent for Aunt Edith? How could he subject her to the care of such a woman? Did he not know that she would be kept as far away from horses as possible while under her aunt's tutelage? No. That was unacceptable. She could not go to stay with her aunt. Not even for a season.

Why just imagine the sort of gentleman Aunt Edith would deem acceptable? He would likely not be the sort who would allow his wife to race her horse along the open field, the was for certain.

"That is not possible." Aunt Edith had finally found her voice. "There was no word of such a thing sent to me by my brother. I do not know what your game is young man, but it will not involve my niece." She turned to Addie. "I think it best if we were to leave tomorrow before you are taken with any other indecorous notions."

"Marrying a gentleman is not indecorous," Addie protested.

"It is if he is a gentleman who sees nothing wrong with how you are dressed and claims to be betrothed to you when your father has only just passed." She shook her head. "Why he is likely eager to claim your fortune."

"You have a fortune?" Mr. Eldridge settled back in his chair and tossed one leg over the other.

It was an action that did not go without a widening of her aunt's eyes. Aunt Edith was clearly affronted by such casual behaviour that did not give her words the weight she believed they deserved.

"I do," Addie replied. "I am sure you and James can discuss that when you go over the marriage papers."

"Marriage papers? There will be no marriage papers!"

"I have a fortune as well," Mr. Eldridge replied, completely ignoring Aunt Edith, "though to be perfectly honest, it is not as much as my sister thinks it should be."

It was as if Mr. Eldridge was purposefully taunting her aunt.

"Your sister?"

Aunt Edith was most certainly out of sorts for she tended to parrot things when shocked and displeased.

"Yes. She has a very good understanding of Stonegate's accounts, you see."

"I do not see. It is not proper." She turned to James. "You will not allow this man to marry our charge."

Addie leaned forward. "What do you mean by *our* charge?" Those words sounded ominous, as if somehow Aunt Edith had been granted permission to make choices about Addie's life.

"Your brother and I have been appointed to care for you, child, and it is a duty I do not and will not take lightly." Aunt Edith straightened a glove. "I, of course, did not realize that I would be taking you on as my ward so soon, but I have been preparing. You will make an excellent match and never want for a thing."

"I have made a match," Addie protested. A very good match. With a gentleman who stirred her heart and passions and reminded her a great deal of her father. There could be no better match for her.

"I know nothing of Mr. Eldridge and am not inclined to accept him."

"I know about Mr. Eldridge and have already approved his petition," James inserted. "I am certain that you could not find a more fitting match for Addie. Why, Mr. Eldridge commands a good estate and a stable which boasts some of the best horses in the land."

"And Miss Atwood has accepted," Mr. Eldridge added. "To break an engagement is not a trifling matter."

He really was very good at taking up a scheme and playing it out. Addie had to admire him for such a skill.

"I see no papers. No one knows you are betrothed."

"I will make certain they know." Addie folded her arms and glowered at her aunt. "Who will marry me then, when I have treated Mr. Eldridge so shabbily? He is not an unknown in town." Or, at least, she assumed he was not unknown if Tom knew him.

"No, no, indeed, I am not. If a man knows anything about horses, they know my estate and my name."

Thankfully, she had been correct in her assumption.

"And, should I marry a gentleman who wishes to do business with Mr. Eldridge – say to purchase a horse for his curricle – I dare say he would not be able to acquire that horse from Mr. Eldridge."

"Nor from anyone who wishes to retain ties to my stables," Mr. Eldridge added, much to Addie's delight. "He would find himself quite horseless or in possession of some broken-down beast." He shook his head. "That would certainly not do for one such as Miss Atwood."

He was fighting for her and with her. She would sigh and admire him for such if it were not for her aunt still looking down her nose at everyone in the room.

Aunt Edith's nostrils flared, but she said nothing to Mr. Eldridge. Instead, she turned to James and seemed to change the subject entirely. "I assume there will be a reading of the will, will there not be?"

"Yes, of course," James answered, "but it will have to wait until after I have returned from Newmarket. Silverthorne's horses must make an appearance and hopefully be successful. The estate depends upon it."

"And when is that?"

"Two weeks and three days from today," James replied. "I and Addie are going to Newmarket for a week ahead of the races and then, will return a few days after."

"I am afraid I cannot allow Adela to travel with you."

"She is my sister!"

"And my niece, whom I should like to see well-matched, and I assume you are travelling with this –" she waved her hand in Robert's direction, "gentleman."

"Yes," James replied. "And we will be staying at his estate. I need Addie to come with me. She knows the horses better than I since I have been at school."

"A lady is not needed for horses."

"I am going," Addie stated. "With or without permission from either of you, I am going. Father and I used to go to the races every year. I will honor his memory even if you will not."

"Such willfulness!" her aunt cried. "I will not have it. You and I will remain here at Silverthorne until your father's will has been read and all the details regarding your future are laid before one and all."

Was her aunt not listening? Addie was not going to stay here while Damon, Mr. Eldridge, and James traveled to Suffolk.

"I think you should change your clothes," Aunt Edith said to Addie when the tea service was brought in. "A lady does not have tea while in breeches." Her aunt rose and claimed the teapot as if it was hers. "Go on, or there will not be a cup of hot tea remaining."

"She will drink it as she is."

James's firm tone surprised Addie. Her brother rarely sounded angry and never authoritative.

"Father's death has been trying for us both," he continued. "Addie has not eaten properly, and I will not have you withholding even a cup of tea from her." He stood. "Take your seat, Aunt Edith. I believe, I am master of this estate, and you are not its mistress. And," he continued, "until I have heard it from the solicitor's lips at the reading of the will, you are not Addie's guardian. I will see to her care."

Addie could not remember a time when she had felt so proud of her brother.

"It is in the will. Your father said it was."

"I will not argue that," James continued as he took their aunt by the elbow and steered her to a chair. "I just will not accept it until I have heard the will."

"I have a letter."

"Which I would be interested to read, but Addie is not your charge until the will is read, for it must be stated in the will to be binding." He had begun pouring the tea. "Milk?" he asked Addie.

"Please."

The milk was added, and Addie was given the first cup. Their aunt had to wait until last, which did nothing to make her any less-pleased.

~*~*~

"We will be ready to leave in the morning," James said to Robert when the three of them stood on the drive waiting for Robert's horse to be brought up from the stables. He glanced back at the house. "Are you both certain you wish to marry? I must say I was taken by surprise at the announcement."

"I could think of no other way to avoid Aunt Edith. You know how she is."

"Does that mean Eldridge is only a means of escape?"

Addie could feel the heat rising to her cheeks. "No."

"My question remains. Are you both certain you wish to marry?"

Was that uncertainty in Mr. Eldridge's eyes? How was she to answer? It was not as if she wished to force Mr. Eldridge into marriage. However, they did seem to be well-matched. They had fallen into an easy friendship, and then, well, there had been that kiss which spoke of more than mere friendship. He had seemed eager enough to pursue her earlier.

"I... I am not opposed to the idea. If I were, I would not have suggested it."

"But you did not suggest it," James said.

"Yes, I did."

"She did," Mr. Eldridge agreed. "And with it she gave me a most speaking look, begging for assistance. As you know from our conversation earlier, I had hoped to court your sister. Therefore, I am not opposed to marrying her."

Not opposed was not the same as being delighted by the possibility. Of course, had she not also used those same words?

"I readily admit that I had not given marriage to Mr. Eldridge –"

"Robert," Mr. Eldridge corrected with a smile.

"I had not given marriage to Robert too much thought until today." Her cheeks were growing quite warm. "However, I find the idea to be..." She blew out a breath. Admitting she liked a gentleman to that gentleman while in the presence of her brother was not exactly comfortable. "very agreeable."

James took her hand. "I am glad to hear it."

"As am I." Mr. Eldridge – er — Robert was smiling broadly. Perhaps he had said not opposed with his words, but his expression certainly said delighted.

"You need to be certain, absolutely, completely certain," James pressed. "I will ask you both again tomorrow, but for now I am satisfied. However, if you still look upon this arrangement as favourable on the morrow, you should know that I intend to see you wed before we return to Silverthorne. Our aunt has no idea what you need to be happy, Addie. While I might not have been the best brother in the past, I will be hanged if I see you tied to any chap she puts forward when a perfectly acceptable one seems happy to have you." He lifted his sister's and extended it to Mr. Eldridge. "I am trusting you with her."

"I feel the weight of such an honour."

Addie smiled to be called an honour. How could she not? It made her feel treasured.

"And now I am going into the house so that you might converse in private."

"Thank you," Addie called to her brother. He was most certainly no longer being a ninny. She smiled. He might have gambled away her horse, but, having heard how he had spoken to their aunt and now knowing his plans to see to her happiness, she knew he was no longer the same foolish person who had wagered where he could not win. If parting with Damon meant reclaiming her brother and gaining Mr. Eldridge, it nearly seemed a worthy sacrifice. Nearly.

He turned, looked at her, and said, "I owe you far more than this" before continuing to the house.

"Do you truly wish to marry me?" Robert asked.

Addie nodded. "I like you very much."

"Enough to put up with my foolishness for a lifetime?"

"Yes." She doubted he was all that foolish. Perhaps he had once been, but he did not seem to be now.

"Then, I shall go home to Mansfield and proclaim the happy news to my sister and Bertram." He paused. "Do you wish for Miss Price to know?"

"Oh, yes, she must know." It was sweet of him to remember her friend.

"I will see that she is informed."

His horse stood before them.

"Until tomorrow," he said, lifting her hand to his lips.

She stood on the drive until he was out of sight. Then, with a sigh, she turned back to the house and prepared herself to be accosted by her aunt. Tomorrow could not come soon enough.

Chapter 12

Just over a day later, Robert helped a road-weary Miss Atwood from her carriage when it arrived at Stonegate. He had not been very long at his estate before the Atwoods arrived, but he had arrived first, as he had pushed on from the last stop ahead of them so that he could warn his staff of the increased number of guests.

True, it was only one more guest than he had included in the express he had sent after arriving back at Mansfield yesterday, but it was one very particular and rather unpleasant guest, who had invited herself along on the journey so that she could watch over her charge.

"I have informed my butler and housekeeper that you are to be their new mistress but that your aunt is not in favour of the match," Robert said as he tucked Addie's hand into the crook of his arm. "They have assured me that Mrs. Bellingham will be given the best service available."

"But not outside of reason," James said. "Aunt Edith may be ignored if she is being unreasonable. Indeed, she can be sent packing if necessary, and I will personally over-see the loading of her carriage."

Robert chuckled. He had heard a little bit about how both James and his sister had retired early last evening to avoid their aunt.

"Were you required to read that letter today?" he asked James.

James's exasperated exhale seemed to be answer enough, but it was not to be.

"I have it in my possession, but I have refused to read it until I choose to read it. I shall not be badgered into it."

"That is understandable." Robert expected he would hear more about it later if James ever decided to read the missive. He motioned to the house before them.

"So, what do you think?"

"It is lovely," Addie replied.

James said something as well, but Robert really did not care what her brother thought of the house. It was Addie's opinion which mattered.

"Do you think you will be happy living here?"

This would soon be her home, and she would be his wife. Standing here next to her and looking at his child-hood home as he was now – through her eyes and not his own, made him see it from a completely new perspective. The fate of this estate would determine the happiness of her life – and his.

Why was breathing becoming such a chore? Who had

placed those plates of iron on his shoulders? He blew out a breath. This must be what Faith had been attempting to get him to understand about the responsibility which accompanied being the master of an estate, the husband of a wife, and the father of children. It was a heavy weight indeed, and not one which could or should be cast aside with ease.

"Yes, I think I will be happy here," Miss Atwood answered. "However, I have only seen the exterior and only the front of the exterior at that, but my first impression is very good."

The weight on his shoulders lifted.

"Might we see the inside?" James asked.

"Oh, of course." He should have offered to take them inside already, but he had to admit that his mind was somewhat addled at the moment. "Do you wish to see to your aunt first?"

Mrs. Bellingham's carriage had just drawn up to where James's had been and the steps would soon be put in place for Aunt Edith's alighting.

"She has servants," James muttered. "And I have no desire to hear her thoughts on what I should or should not be doing. Lead on Eldridge. Lead on."

And so, Robert did.

"Do you suppose that later, perhaps, we could see the stables?" Addie asked as they made their way down the walkway from the drive to the house.

"Tomorrow," James replied before Robert could say a word. "Tonight is for rest and recovery."

"I am well," Addie protested.

"And I would have you stay that way," James retorted. "Besides, if you become ill, you will be left to the care of our aunt while Eldridge and I are out riding."

"Faith is here," Robert inserted. His sister would not hear of Miss Atwood being the sole female at Stonegate. "But I also would not wish for you to become unwell."

Addie's sigh was such a disappointed sound that Robert immediately decided, should some opportunity present itself later, he would sneak her out to the stables — with a properly warm wrap and all that, of course. He wanted to grant her wish to see that Damon was well, but he would not do it without some precautions to keep her well.

"Damon, Pythias, and Hugo are well-tended to," he assured her and was rewarded with a smile and a small thank you. "We will have tea after you have gotten settled in your rooms, and then, I will give you a tour of the house." He escorted her through the arched entry and into the house proper where Faith joined them.

"I will see Miss Atwood to her room," Faith said to her brother.

And so, just as he had gotten her into his home, he was required to give Miss Atwood up, but thankfully, it was only for about half an hour. Then, she joined him for tea in the small yellow drawing room just down the hall from the guest quarters and before you reached the family room. To his delight, she took a seat between him and his sister.

"Is your room to your liking?"

"I like it very much."

"If there are changes you wish to make..." Once again, those plates of iron rested on his shoulders. His need for her to like his home – their home — was nearly overwhelming. "They can be seen to after we marry."

"I am certain that neither my room nor this room needs any changes." Addie smiled at him. "They are quite to my taste."

"They are?" Was she saying what was polite, or was she really pleased with the rooms?

"Yes." She leaned toward him. "I especially like this room since you are here." Her cheeks flushed. "Not that I am saying I would like you to be in my room or that it is lacking because you are not there or..." her voice trailed off. "I was just trying to assure you that I like your home." She blew out a breath. "Not just because it is a fine house, but because it is your home."

Ah, she was content, and he could breathe again without it being a herculean effort.

"This is one of Robert's favourite rooms," Faith said as she handed a cup of tea to him.

"I can see why," Miss Atwood said. "It is so welcoming. I think any lady or gentleman could feel quite safely sequestered and comfortable for a great deal of time in this room." She took a sip of her tea. "That chair by the window seems an excellent place to stitch or read."

"I have not done any stitching in that chair, but I will assure you that it is very comfortable for reading," Robert answered. He would have to see that a second chair was placed near the window so they could sit there together.

"Do you like to read?"

Robert nodded. "And you?"

"Very much."

Robert put his cup down instead of taking a sip. "Regular books, as fits the standard for ladies, or are your tastes more irregular?"

There was still much he did not know about her. He knew her thoughts on the proper care of horses and in which activities she preferred to take part outside of her home. Those were some of the topics they had canvassed while he was helping train Damon and drinking tea in the sitting room at Silverthorne. However, he had little knowledge of her personal likes regarding such things as fashion, décor, and leisurely pastimes.

"To be honest, I enjoy a bit of both. Novels and poetry are excellent ways to while away a few hours, but an occasional book regarding something of educational value is also delightful."

"Do these educational books pertain only to the administration of a house and the care of linens and the like?" He smiled as he put his cup to his lips. He suspected he knew her answer from the way her eyebrows arched.

"I do not confine my perusal of instructional books to those considered *in the female domain*." Her eyes challenged him to condemn her.

"Good." He returned his cup to the table. "I should very much dislike having a wife who was less diverse in her interest than the female with whom I have been longest acquainted."

Miss Atwood's brow furrowed.

"My sister," he clarified. "Faith is trying at times, but I quite like being able to speak with her on a great range of topics."

"But I do not know if I know as much as she!" Addie cried.

"You do not have to," Robert assured her. He had not meant to cause her any unease.

"I have not studied investments." Her nose wrinkled in an adorable fashion as she said the word investments. "However, I am certain I could learn about them."

He had no doubt she could. Miss Atwood struck him as a lady who conquered whatever challenge she set before herself. In that way, she was also a great deal like his sister.

"Addie is keen." James inserted but unfortunately, at least, for Robert, could not elaborate more on the excessively diverting topic of his sister as his aunt had just arrived for tea and was evidently not the sort who slipped into a room unnoticed.

"This is a small room," Mrs. Bellingham said upon entering. "However, it does get good light."

Robert was uncertain if that meant this room was acceptable or not, so he settled on that she found it marginally acceptable.

"It could use a bit of updating," she added.

Or perhaps she found it a bit less than marginally acceptable.

"Do try to be polite," James scolded. "Just because you are not pleased with Addie's future husband, does not give you permission to be cantankerous. You do not need to stay here, you know."

"And where else am I to stay? I must keep an eye on my charge."

"She is not your charge."

"But she will be, and she must know how to properly evaluate a home for when she actually finds a gentleman worth marrying. The fact that this room has not been updated in some time suggests that funds are not as abundant as they should be."

"Or," James countered, "it means that Mr. Eldridge is fiscally responsible and does not toss his money away on bits of fluff."

"Bits of fluff," Mrs. Bellingham muttered.

"Actually," Robert said, "my sister updated this room

not less than five years ago. Not much was done, as Faith is no spendthrift, but, to be honest, I have not, to this point in my life, been all that concerned with how a room looked beyond the fact that I liked it. Why change something if it does not need changing?" That he was more interested in spending his money on other pursuits was not worth noting at present.

"Indeed?"

She was looking down her nose at him, but she had not lectured him on not being bothered with décor and furnishings.

"Your sister has traditional tastes."

"Only in décor," Robert assured his guest. "She is less traditional in her outlook on life."

"I believe in making changes where they are needed," Faith said.

"I like tradition," Mrs. Bellingham said.

That was no surprise!

"I am not opposed to tradition," Robert said, "but I am not tied to it either."

An eyebrow rose while her lips pursed.

"Nor is Addie, which makes Mr. Eldridge a most acceptable choice for her," James challenged. "And until I have heard you appointed as guardian in my father's will, your opinion on the eligibility of a match for Addie is of no consequence."

Cups clinked softly against saucers for a moment before

James added, "I dare say your opinion will not matter all that much to me after either."

Mrs. Bellingham huffed and applied herself to her tea.

Again, silence ruled the room for a moment.

"What do you know of marriage?" Mrs. Bellingham said. "You have only just finished school. You have very little knowledge of what it takes to provide for a family. How then, shall you be able to decipher who is or who is not a good match for Adela?"

So the woman did care for her niece's wellbeing in a roundabout fashion.

"Do you think I am incapable of knowing my mind?" Miss Atwood asked. "Do you think I have not seen what kind of effort goes into the management of a home and estate? Who do you think cared for the things my mother did before she grew too ill to do them? Who do you think saw to the estate while Father lay in bed?"

"Not your brother," Mrs. Bellingham answered.

"No, not my brother because he had responsibilities elsewhere." She fixed her eyes on that brother who was looking rather chagrined. "But, Aunt Edith, who do you think knows better what I need to be happy than the brother who saw to my happiness as often as he could while we were growing up and before he had to leave for school?" She turned to look at her aunt. "Not you. I do not know why my father gave my care to you. We have so little in common."

"Perhaps," Faith said softly, "if I may intrude, it was because your father knew your aunt could introduce you to a certain level of society that your brother, being young, might not yet be able to do. Your aunt might be your father's way of providing assistance not only to you but also to your brother."

Robert thought he had long since overcome being amazed at his sister's astuteness, but, at the moment, he found her wisdom inspiring.

"And maybe, Mrs. Bellingham, your brother knew that his son was capable of selecting a capable and even excellent husband for his sister because he knew his daughter would make well-thought-out choices. Could it not be possible that he likely knew his son would see to the well-being of his sister for he had seen the love the two shared for each other?"

Mrs. Bellingham's eyes roamed up and down Faith as if she were assessing her. "I will allow that it is possible."

Faith smiled. "Then, could you, please, attempt to find some good in my brother? I assure you he has been foolish plenty of times while growing up – as most are — but his heart is good. I have never once doubted that he would put me in danger."

"Never, you say?"

Faith nodded. "Never. Though I lectured him beyond reason for his errors, as any good older sister should."

Mrs. Bellingham smiled? She actually knew how to form such an expression? Robert was both shocked and pleased.

"Well, then, I shall give him a chance." Mrs. Bellingham shifted her gaze to Robert. "Do not disappoint me, young man, for I am still not inclined to accept you."

Chapter 13

A breeze bent the grass and pulled at Addie's skirt and bonnet. A blanket of grey clouds could be seen in the distance. Tomorrow, it would likely be too wet to race, and so it had been decided that one more pass down the course at Stonegate before returning to the stables would be an excellent idea.

Damon snorted and tossed his head. Even after having run as much as he already had today, he was eager for the race to begin. He had always been eager for a gallop, but since he had been training with Mr. Eldridge, that desire had increased. He was born to race. A love of racing flowed in his blood and twitched in every fiber of his being. Seeing him fly down the course was exhilarating, though not as thrilling as riding him while he flew would be. However, Addie was not to be granted the excitement of riding Damon, nor would she be given the chance to run Hugo against him. Since arriving at Stonegate, Addie had been relegated to watching the racing rather than participating.

It made sense, she told herself. She would not be riding

in the race at the end of the week. Someone else would be and that someone needed time to become familiar with Hugo. But no matter how much she told herself it was what had to happen, she could not bring herself to be completely happy about it.

She caught Damon's face in her hands and kissed his nose. "Fly like the wind," she whispered. "You must win." She gave Damon's nose one more kiss and repeated her instructions to him. Oh, she would miss him – if their plan did not work and it came to that, that is.

"Must you put your mouth on that beast?"

Aunt Edith was less than pleased to once again be standing next to the track watching a race. It was not where she thought a lady should be. It was one thing to don a new hat and take in a race at a proper racing facility, but to stand out here in a field, as she called it, was another thing altogether.

"Yes, I must," Addie replied. She smiled up at Robert. "Are you going to win?"

"I am shocked you should even ask." There was a twinkle in his eye. "I do enjoy winning."

"As do I," Addie agreed.

"You are not racing," Aunt Edith scolded. "Not even for a lark."

Addie rolled her eyes, and Robert chuckled. Aunt Edith had been absolutely horrified to hear that Addie had been racing against her brother and Mr. Eldridge. Proper young ladies did not do such things. Racing was dangerous and rather hoydenish.

Addie did not agree, of course. Nor did Robert. This did nothing to raise Mr. Eldridge in the eyes of Aunt Edith. In fact, once she learned that Miss Eldridge also enjoyed an occasional race, she proclaimed herself to be utterly scandalized.

"Do not encourage her, Mr. Eldridge," she added.

"Father did not mind my racing," Addie countered.

"Your father..." Aunt Edith shook her head but said no more.

Addie breathed a sigh of relief. There were only so many times she could listen to how her father should have sought help raising a young lady well before it was too late. This would then dissolve into grousing over how she was ever going to make Addie presentable in time for next season, which, in turn, would set James's teeth on edge and lead to an argument between aunt and nephew. Needless to say, the past three days at Stonegate had been trying.

"I will see you after I win," Robert said with a wink. He was very good at ignoring Aunt Edith's diatribes and taunting her with his unruffled appearance. However, Addie knew that he was not as complacent as he appeared, for she had heard him grumbling about her aunt to Damon on more than one occasion when she had arrived at the stables to meet him.

Addie was coming to love the stables even more than

she already did but for a reason wholly unrelated to horses, for the stables were a place to which Aunt Edith would not venture. They were also the place where Robert had collected on his wins each day. He would hand her a brush to help him see to either Hugo or Damon, and then, when the grooms would conveniently find work elsewhere and the stall door was closed, he would toss the brushes to the side and gather her into his arms. She sighed. Those times were the only ones where any thoughts about horses or races being lost were nowhere near Addie's mind.

"I will look forward to it," she called after him as he joined her brother who was riding Pythias and Stonegate's jockey who was riding Hugo. The comment was met with a wide grin and bow of his head as he touched his hat.

Was there anything more wonderful in the whole world than being loved by a gentleman such as he? Addie was not certain there was. Not even racing across an open field on Damon's back could compare to spending time with Mr. Eldridge.

James reined Pythias into line between Hugo and Damon. Pythias was doing well, but he was a trifle skittish at times. However, of the three horses lining up to race, he was the one who was most likely to cause her lips to go without a victory kiss. Hugo was also a threat, but not like Pythias. Pythias's youth and potential continued to amaze her and Mr. Eldridge as well. Both of them were hopeful that their plan to entice Mr. Camden into taking Pythias over Damon would work. It was only Pythias's wariness and inexperience which posed a threat to their plan. Camden might not wish for a horse who was so green.

Camden had been seen in Newmarket, according to what James had heard at the Jockeys Club, but he had not yet come to Stonegate to see how Damon was progressing. Addie expected he would arrive soon, as the race was not many days away. She could not imagine anyone, let alone a man intent upon winning bets like Mr. Camden was, not checking on the likelihood of a win before the day of a race. However, she was not unhappy the man had not yet appeared.

As this last practice race of the day began, Addie divided her attention between Mr. Eldridge on Damon and James on Pythias. It did look as if Damon might not win this race. Not only was Pythias growing stronger, James had also improved his techniques. The two of them were moving so well together.

"There is something going on up there," Aunt Edith said, pulling Addie's attention away from the race.

"Where?"

"Up on the left near the thicket."

"It is likely just some animal," Miss Eldridge assured them.

And she was right for just a moment after she had said it, a hare bounded out of the thicket and onto the track.

The sudden appearance of the creature startled Pythias, and he shied to the right.

"Oh no!" Addie was running down the track before Pythias collided with Damon.

With a scream that rose above the shouts of riders, Damon stumbled and fell, tossing Robert to the side of the racecourse.

"Oh, please, get up," she begged with what breath was not being used to propel her forward. "Get up. Please, get up!" She could not lose either of them. She simply could not.

Damon's head lifted, and he attempted to rise but could not. Mr. Eldridge was sitting up and attempting to make his way back to Damon. Clearly neither had been left uninjured.

She tore her eyes away from them to search for her brother, who was still bringing Pythias under control a short distance away.

Reaching Damon, who was lying very still, Addie dropped down next to him and rubbed his side while surveying his limbs. It was as she feared. His leg was bleeding where a bone had torn through the skin.

"No, no, no," she muttered as she fell on his belly.

"Addie." Faith rubbed her back.

"He is gone," Addie said between tears.

"Not yet," Faith replied.

"But soon," Addie lifted her head. "He should not suffer. I know how it is."

"As do I," Faith assured her. "Do you wish to stay with him until..."

Addie shook her head. "I cannot. I know it must be done, but I cannot be here." A hand grasped hers.

"Addie." Robert had made it to where Damon lay. "I..." He shook his head, unable to speak.

She squeezed his hand. "You could not have prevented it."

"I wish I could have," he replied before wincing as he shifted position.

Addie's thoughts were immediately arrested by the sound. Her heart broke for the loss of her horse, but it raced with fear, unlike anything she had ever felt before, when Robert rested himself against Damon's back and seemed to fade away.

She scrambled around Damon to Robert's side. Faith was running her hands along her brother's limbs.

"Is he –?" Addie could not form the word alive as her fear choked her.

"He has only swooned."

Oh, that was good. Addie could breath. She took Robert's hand which was closest to her and lifted it to her lips as her relief at his being alive set fresh tears falling.

"I cannot feel any broken bones," Faith assured her. "However, that does not mean he has not sprained something." Faith lifted her skirt and tore at her petticoat with a pocketknife she had found in the pocket of her brother's jacket. "Hold his head while I wrap this around it. If we can stop the flow of blood, he may come to."

Addie did as she was told.

"Will it be enough?" she whispered.

Faith blew out a breath. "I pray it is."

Robert moaned but his eyes remained closed. Still, Addie sighed with relief to hear him.

Faith looked up at the two grooms who had joined them. "He is ready to go home as soon as the cart is brought over here." Then with a heavy sigh, she sat back on her heels looking drawn.

"He will be well," Addie assured her. "He has to be."

Faith replied with a tight smile and a nod of her head.

Addie moved to wrap an arm around Faith's shoulders as the grooms lifted Robert from where he was and carried him a distance to meet the cart.

"Do be careful with him," Aunt Edith barked at the grooms who were moving Robert. "Is there someone to go for the surgeon? And how shall we get you home?" She added looking at Addie and Faith.

"We will walk."

Aunt Edith huffed. "Walk! I dare say it will be too taxing, though I don't suppose there are too many other options. You there, with the cart!" She held her hand up to hale the driver. "Be quick in returning. We will meet you in the way."

"I have my horse," Faith said. "Addie could ride with me."

"I do not think so," Aunt Edith said as she circled Addie and Faith who had risen from the ground. Her eyes swept up and down them, and she stopped to fiddle with Faith's sleeve and to pull at a wrinkle in Addie's skirt. "You have just had a terrible shock, the both of you. I will not hear of your riding. Why what if you should swoon?" She shook her head and clucked her tongue. "It is bad enough to have one in need of the surgeon, we do not need another." She dabbed at her eyes.

Her manner and words were brusque, but she was not without feeling, even if she did believe in keeping her emotions locked away. "Why, your father," she said to Addie, "and your brother," she said to Faith, "would not forgive me for allowing you to put yourself in harm's way." She blew out a breath and shook her head. "Indeed, Mr. Eldridge would see me tossed out twice if I allowed harm to come to either of you." She presented her arms to them. "One on each side, please."

"Thank you," Addie whispered.

"It is nothing," her aunt replied with a smile.

But it was not nothing. It was a great deal more than nothing to be cared for by Aunt Edith, even if it was done in a commanding fashion.

"James," she said, leveling a hard stare at him as he sat on his horse with Pythias's reins in one hand and his other tucked in his lap as if it needed protecting. "Allow us to be a distance away before you do what needs to be done."

Addie pressed her lips together, tucking them between her teeth and biting down on them to keep them from trembling. Her tears would not stay confined, however.

"I will have the surgeon wait to take a look at you, James," Aunt Edith added before leading Addie and Faith in the direction of the cart path.

As they entered the cart path with a row of trees between them and the racecourse, a gunshot rang out, and Addie whispered a goodbye to Damon in her heart.

Chapter 14

Oh, his head was throbbing, but it seemed as if the sun was shining. What had he done to wake with such a painful head? Robert lifted a hand to rub his temples and gasped at the pain such a movement caused.

"Take care, young man. We cannot have the surgeon out here every day to redo what he has done."

Slowly, very slowly, Robert opened one eye and then the other.

"Good, you are awake."

Mrs. Bellingham was standing next to his bed and peering down at him, and she was not scowling. He closed his eyes, pinching them closed tightly, and then, opened them again. No, she was still there, and she was still not scowling.

"You have given us quite the scare, Mr. Eldridge. A full day of being insensible is far too much, young man."

She was scolding so perhaps this was reality and not some horrid dream. Chair legs scraped across the floor, causing Robert to wince.

"I have decided you are acceptable." Mrs. Bellingham plopped herself down on the chair she had drawn close.

"You have?"

She nodded. "I have told neither Adela nor James about my decision, but it is made."

Robert doubted any decision once made by Mrs. Bellingham was changeable. Although, she had at one time declared him unacceptable, so perhaps her decisions were subject to modification? Not that he wished her to alter her way of thinking about him at present.

"Adela could do worse."

A resounding vote of confidence if ever he heard one. He would chuckle if he were not afraid it might offend his visitor.

"However, I am nearly positive she could do no better."

"Thank you?" Robert was not certain if that was a compliment of his person or a disparagement of Addie.

"How is your head?"

"Sore."

"That is as it should be."

Indeed? Was there perhaps not a better nurse to be stationed at his side? Perhaps one who would show some pity for his aching head?

"You sustained quite a blow to your skull. The surgeon thought you had likely knocked your brain about a good bit and that it would take a while to clear."

That explained the pain in his head.

"And my arm?" There was a bandage around his throbbing elbow.

"The bones are not broken, but it appears your elbow is sprained. It will need to be rested for a month or more." She gave him a severe look. "There will be no riding until it is healed. I will not have my niece marrying a cripple because he is too stubborn to do what is best for him."

"Yes, ma'am." What else did one say to such a thing, especially when it was accompanied by that look. Mrs. Bellingham would make a terrifyingly good headmistress of a school – and not just a girls' school. Robert was certain the woman could glare many young boys into doing as they were told.

She smiled. "Good. I am happy to hear you are a cooperative patient." She smoothed her skirt. "As I understand it, you have a few other bruises and a scrape or two, but the head and the arm are your most pressing injuries. The horse, of course, did not fare so well."

With her last statement, the accident came rushing into his memory — vivid and excruciating.

"Where is Addie?" He needed to see her, to know that she was well. He could not imagine the grief she was feeling at having lost Damon in such a fashion.

"She and your sister will be allowed to see you as soon as I am done."

"Yes, ma'am."

"Now, about my decision to find you acceptable."

Her disquieting glare was back.

"We had a call from a gentleman named Mr. Camden yesterday."

Oh. Robert closed his eyes.

"Ah, I see you know of whom I speak."

"I do."

"He is a most despicable gentleman."

"That he is."

"I wish to thank you for putting yourself and your horse at risk for my nephew." She smiled again.

Robert was not sure which was more unsettling, her glare or her smile. The glare seemed as if it belonged on her face. The smile was less at home there.

"I have had the full story, and that is why I have decided you are the best choice for Adela. Not every gentleman would throw himself into a scheme to see his new acquaintances were safe from the likes of that slippery eel of a fellow." She tipped her head. "I am only still concerned about one thing."

"And that would be?" Robert asked cautiously.

"You knew who Mr. Camden was. Therefore, I assume you are given to gambling."

Ah. Yes. That would concern him too if he were her. "I *was* given to gambling. I am no longer." He held up a finger on his uninjured arm. "Not that I am not opposed to a small wager now and then, but never to excess. My frivolousness nearly cost me the life of a good friend."

"So your sister told me." Mrs. Bellingham leaned toward him. "But she seems to think you have changed your ways, and I must say, I approve of her way of thinking on such things as seeing to one's future. Perhaps not to the point of taking up a man's work of investing — but retrenching and the like. She is very practical, she is."

"That she is, along with being rather wise and excellent at scolding me."

Mrs. Bellingham's smile reached her eyes. "That is a very good quality for an elder sister to have." Her head tipped. "Except perhaps once her younger brother had married and started his own family. Then, it never goes well to attempt to scold him into behaving or seeing that his daughter acts like a proper young lady should. Not that Adela is improper, but her love of horses..." She shook her head. "Ah, well, it seems my brother knew what he was about. He always told me that he would wager his whole estate on the notion that a head full of horses would serve her well in finding a good match. I thought he was mad for thinking so, but it seems he was not and has, thanks to you, won that wager." She sighed. "It is just too bad he is not here to hear me say so."

She stood. "That friend of yours who you almost killed, Mr. Bertram, has arrived just this morning. I will tell him you will see him after I have allowed my niece to see you." She shook her head. "She is rather headstrong, Mr.

Eldridge, but so is your sister, so I expect you are prepared for such a wife." She smiled and winked at him. Winked!

"Thank you, Mrs. Bellingham. I am certain Addie and I will get on quite well."

She nodded. "I do not doubt it, and if we are to be related, I suppose you should get used to calling me Aunt Edith." Her brows flicked upward. "My niece has no parents left, and my brother did ask me to see to her. Therefore, I intend to visit at least once a year, though perhaps more frequently."

Oh, well, that was something to look forward to, Robert thought wryly as *Aunt Edith* left the room. However, the beautiful face that appeared at his door on the heels of her aunt's departure was worth a yearly disagreeable visitor. His sister, who was next to Addie, waved but closed the door without entering. Aunt Edith would be displeased, but Robert was not.

"Are you well?" he asked, pushing himself up to a sitting position.

"I am not the one who has been insensible for nearly a day," she replied.

"No, but you are the one who lost a horse. A bumped head and bruised body are nothing to that."

She shook her head. "A horse is not as important as you." She propped on the edge of his bed and took his hand.

"Be careful with that arm. I have been instructed to rest

it for a month, and if I fail to do what I should, your aunt will withdraw her consent for me to marry you."

Addie's eyes grew wide. "My aunt gave you her consent?"

Robert nodded. His head hurt a whole lot less conversing with Addie than it had during her aunt's interview.

"It appears my taking part in rescuing your brother from Camden was enough to make me acceptable."

"Oh!" Addie cried. "She was excessively displeased to discover the sort of trouble into which James had gotten himself, and she was not impressed one bit by Mr. Camden. She gave him quite the dressing down about his manners and the way he spoke to ladies!"

"And I missed it?"

Addie laughed. "You did. However, he intends to see you at the race, so you have not missed the pleasure of his presence entirely."

He would be glad to have seen the last of Camden. "Did he take Pythias?"

"Only if he wins."

"James will see that he does."

Addie shook her head. "James wrenched his shoulder. I do not think he will be able to race. He has sent for Stuart."

"What if he does not win?"

"Then James will owe Camden twice what he did, and, of course, Hugo will also become Mr. Camden's."

"One hundred and fifty pounds and Hugo?"

Addie nodded.

"He did not have seventy-five pounds." It was just like Camden to deepen the hole into which a fellow had fallen rather than lifting him out. However, he was surprised that Camden had not just taken Hugo since Robert was no longer going to be racing.

"He did not just take Hugo?"

"Aunt Edith would not hear of it."

Perhaps Aunt Edith was not so very bad after all.

"Pythias will win," Addie assured him.

Robert blew out a breath. "I hope you are correct."

She leaned towards him and placed a hand on his cheek. "I will not have you losing Hugo. Pythias will win."

He covered her hand with his good one and, turning his head, placed a kiss in her palm. "You cannot guarantee that."

"Stuart is good. You know how well he rode when we were at Silverthorne. He was as good if not better than James." She smiled at him. "He is not you, but he is nearly as good. And, he will not be riding against you, so his chances are much better."

Robert was still not completely convinced, but he did like hearing her praise of him and the quick kiss which accompanied it.

"Will Camden think my rider is not riding as hard as he can if Hugo does not win?" He asked after drawing her back for another, longer kiss. "It is not advantageous to me to have Hugo win as the agreement stands."

He blinked. "It never has been." Why had he not seen that before?

"It has never been to Camden's advantage for Damon to win. Unless..." His brow furrowed. "Unless, he was placing money on Damon to win – enough to make up for whatever he lost last year, plus whatever he hopes to make this year. It was always about throwing the race. Only, he knew I would never do that. Therefore, he needed me to ride the winner because another rider might be less aggressive. And a less aggressive rider on Hugo would almost guarantee that my riding a worthy racer – one that I had hand selected for him — would secure him his money. Or –" A horrifying thought came to mind.

"What was the first thing Camden said when he arrived?"

Addie looked puzzled. "He said he had heard that James owed him a horse."

"And after that? Did he demand Hugo?"

"Not until after James offered him Pythias in Damon's place."

"Why did he not take Pythias?" If Camden were truly interested in a horse as payment, he would have taken Pythias. Surely, he would have. Why make it dependent upon a win?

"He did not wish for a horse who shied at rabbits."

That was interesting. "Had James told him about the hare?"

She nodded.

Robert sank back on his pillows. It could still be true that Camden was behind the sudden arrival of that hare on the racecourse. Robert had ridden there many times, and yesterday was the first time he had seen a hare there. Pheasants he had seen, as well as a deer or two, but never a hare.

"What are you thinking?" Addie asked.

"It may never have been about me winning. It might have always been about my losing and him taking Hugo from me." He shook his head. But why kill the horse who could guarantee him a payday?

He blew out a breath as a possible answer hit him. It was likely not his plan to kill Damon, but rather to just injure him so that he could not ride and would have to forfeit Hugo.

"I am not entirely certain what twisted game Camden is playing, but if we are to win, we need to keep a close eye on Pythias and Stuart." And pray that no hares decided to attend the race.

Chapter 15

On race day, Addie took her place at the rail next to Robert. His injured arm was tucked safely inside a sling, but his other arm was wrapped snuggly in hers. This would be the first of many races they would attend together, though likely he would not be here beside her as he was now but rather he would be mounted on a horse preparing to win. Faith stood at her other side, and Tom next to her. James had the great privilege to be his aunt's escort.

"Camden," Robert called. "Join us."

The gentleman turned from wherever it was he was headed and made his way towards them.

"I have a thousand pounds for you."

Camden looked at Robert warily. Addie's mind was echoing the same sentiment. Why was Robert offering Camden a thousand pounds?

"It was Hugo or a thousand pounds if you remember."

"That was if you were riding. A new arrangement has been reached."

"Mr. Eldridge was not present to agree to that," Aunt Edith said. "A proper gentleman would allow for the gentleman with whom he is wagering to agree or decline the wager." She gave Mr. Camden a withering look. "Not that I count you as a proper gentleman."

Mr. Camden's eyes narrowed, just as Aunt Edith waved to someone.

"Who is that?" James asked.

"That is Mrs. Holdsworth and her husband. Miss Eldridge, Adela, and I met her yesterday when I was getting flowers for my hat. Is not her hat exquisite?"

"Mrs. Holdsworth, you say?" Mr. Camden shifted uneasily.

"Yes, do you know her? I am sure if you have been around these parts very much at all you likely do. Her husband is the magistrate." Aunt Edith fluttered her lashes at Mr. Camden. "Much like my husband's cousin on his mother's side is. Is it not wonderful to find people so far from your home and yet with whom you have so much in common?"

"Yes, yes, I am certain it is," Mr. Camden agreed quickly.

"About our arrangement," Robert prodded.

"Very well, a thousand pound or your horse if Atwood's replacement wins."

"No, no. It was if he lost."

"But it is not the same horse," Camden hissed.

"No, but he is just as good if not better. Atwood has

been training him along side me, so I know of what I speak. You do still trust my evaluation of a horse, do you not?"

"Oh, Mrs. Holdsworth," Aunt Edith called with a glance over her shoulder at Mr. Camden. "I was just commenting on your hat. It goes very well with your pelisse. You were quite right to go with the yellow ribbon."

"Of course, I do," Camden snapped.

Addie smiled. Her aunt might be a demanding woman who did not have a great love of horses, but she was also a rather cunning one.

"Then, we have an agreement," Robert said. "Pythias wins, and you get to take him home assured that he is indeed a winner, while I get to keep my money and my horse."

"Are you planning to throw the race, Eldridge?" Camden asked.

"I am not the sort of fellow to ever do that," Robert replied.

"I had thought as much," Camden muttered with a glance at where Aunt Edith stood, conversing with her new friend about fripperies and such.

"To prove my character," Robert said, "I have another wager to make with you."

"I am listening." Mr. Camden seemed to forget Mrs. Holdsworth and Aunt Edith in his eagerness to hear about Robert's bet. To be truthful, Addie was also quite interested to hear it.

"I am so confident in Pythias to win and Hugo's ability to come close to beating him, that I will give you one hundred pounds," he nodded to Faith who handed Mr. Camden an envelope, "and you only have to return that to me if Pythias does not win and Hugo does not place second. Should Pythias win, and Hugo comes anywhere lower than second, you keep the money. If Pythias loses and Hugo is either higher or lower than second, you still keep that hundred pounds. Both conditions must be met for you to have to give that money back to me. Do we have an agreement?"

Camden turned the envelope over in his hand.

"Both horses must finish the race," Robert added.

Oh, he was clever! No wonder he was offering a hundred pounds. He was attempting to ensure that Mr. Camden would do nothing to cause Pythias to lose. However, Mr. Camden did not look convinced that it was the best offer.

"How much would you take for Pythias? He is a skittish horse and could be a liability if not handled properly," Robert said. "He has to be worth at least seventy-five before he has run the race, and I would be willing to go higher at the end when he has won."

"What are you up to, Eldridge?" Camden asked skeptically.

"Pythias is good. Very good," Robert replied. "Atwood is not going to part with him if he loses because a horse with the green talent that Pythias has would be a boon to Silverthorne. However, you may not be as interested in housing and training a young stallion, so I thought I would offer to take him off your hands."

Camden's lips quirked up into a calculating smile. "A thousand pounds now or twice that at the end of the race."

Robert watched the horses taking their last little run before forming a line to start. "That is a bit excessive."

"But you have it as you have already offered it in place of your horse," Camden pressed.

Robert drew and released a breath. "Tom, what do you think?"

"It is a lot of money," Tom said.

"Not as much as two thousand," Camden inserted.

"Miss Atwood, you know your horses, especially those from Silverthorne's stables," Robert smiled down at her. "Would you say Pythias is capable of bringing my money back to me?"

"Without a doubt." Pythias was young and, barring any injury, had a good number of races left in him to run. Added to that were the fees which could be charged for his services in breeding.

"And would you ride him?"

"Possibly. Though I would rather see my brother riding him."

"He could when he visits," Robert replied.

"Oh, ho!" Camden cried. "You did use that horse – my

horse – to snare yourself a filly just as I said you would." He tapped the envelop he held against his other palm. "You'll want to keep the lady happy. A thousand pounds is not so much to spend for that, now is it?"

"You make a good point." Robert winked at Addie.

He was playing Camden right into his hands! He had been planning to accept the offer from the beginning. This must be why he and Tom had been sequestered in the study for so long yesterday. They must have been playing through the various scenarios of what might happen.

"It is still a great deal of money." He sighed. "However, you have a deal." He nodded at Faith once again, who handed Mr. Camden another envelope. "That is the thousand I had prepared to give you if Pythias lost the race, so the money is yours no matter the result."

"And the skittish stallion is yours if he wins."

Robert extended his hand to Camden, who shook it and ambled away with a pocket full of money, just as the race got underway. That would hopefully be the last Addie ever saw of that man — except maybe once more when they collected both Hugo and Pythias at the end of the race, for Pythias was gaining a good lead, one which Addie knew he would not lose.

~*~*~

"You had best be worth the effort," Addie said later as she stroked Pythias's nose while Robert used his good arm to run a brush along his side. "A groom can do that," she suggested.

"I know," Robert replied, "and I promise to let a groom do the majority of it. However, I believe that an animal will care more for his rider if that rider has first cared for him."

"Do you hear that, Pythias? Mr. Eldridge plans on riding you."

"But not until my arm is healed," Robert said from the other side of the horse.

"You know he is nearly the best rider at Stonegate." Addie peered around Pythias's head and gave Robert a taunting smile.

"You think you can outride me, do you?"

Addie nodded. "If I am wearing breeches."

Robert shook his head and discarded his brush. "Would you like to bet on that, Miss Atwood?"

Addie stuck out her hand. "The winner gets to claim a favour from the loser of the winner's choosing whenever the winner decides to claim it."

Robert hesitated in taking her hand. "Can I trust your honour not to ruin my reputation?"

Addie laughed. "Only until we are married."

He reached to take her hand, but she pulled it back. "Do you promise the same?"

He shrugged. "Most likely."

She laughed.

"I am marrying you whether your reputation is intact or not," he said with a wicked grin.

"Yes, but if you ruin my reputation, Aunt Edith will not be pleased."

He lunged forward and grabbing her hand, pulled her to him. "Your Aunt Edith is rarely pleased."

"Our aunt," Addie corrected. "She will be yours, too." She loved how it felt to be held by him.

"Very well," he kissed her nose. "Our aunt is rarely pleased."

"But I do not think it is wise idea to purposefully taunt her and make her disagreeable. She might decide to stay for an indefinite amount of time to make sure you are treating me well."

She expected him to protest some more, but he did not. Instead, he lowered his head and kissed her. Deeply. Passionately. Teasing her mouth open with his tongue and then tangling it with hers. Pulling back, he kissed her gently. Softly. Leaving her longing for more. Then he rested his head against hers.

"Do you still want me to promise not to ruin your reputation until we are married?" His smile was very self-satisfied.

"I think..." Goodness! He had made her sound breathy and wanton again. "I think I must insist upon it, Mr. Eldridge."

He kissed her lips softly once more. "That is likely wise, but is it what you want?"

"No." The word was out of her mouth before it had passed through her mind.

He backed her up so that she was leaning against the door to Pythias's stall. "I have only one arm to hold you," he explained as he pressed himself against her.

"Robert," she scolded, though she really was not all that shocked or displeased by his actions. However, it was the proper thing to do.

"Addie." He kissed her forehead. "I cannot hold you against me and tangle my hand in your hair back here." He slid his fingers into the bottom portion of her coiffeur. "If I only have one arm. Therefore, I intend to use the door to assist me."

That seemed to make sense, she supposed, though her ability to think rationally was limited at the moment.

"Now, about our wager. I, Robert Eldridge, agree to not ruin your reputation, Adela Atwood, by claiming an intimate favour until you are my wife." He smiled at her. "Do we have an agreement?"

She nodded. Words were really beyond her ability at the moment. His body leaning into hers, his hand in her hair and his lips so close to her were intoxicating.

"Do you still wish to shake hands?" he asked near her ear before he kissed it.

"No." Her voice was once again breathy, and she gasped as he kissed her neck.

"We should marry soon," he murmured.

She was in agreement with that. Hopefully, Aunt Edith would not protest their marrying during a mourning period. Six months would be far too long to wait. Maybe James had gotten the license he had promised to get before they had left Silverthorne. She would have to ask him.

"And likely we should not race until we have." He once again nibbled her neck. He lifted his head and looked into her eyes. "I love you," he whispered.

"And I, you," she replied.

He smiled. "Who would have thought I would find such a perfect woman to love?"

"I am not perfect." Though she did like that he thought so.

"Oh, but you are. You are beautiful. You are smart. You know as much about horses as I do. You love a good race, and you are not opposed to a friendly wager." He kissed her. "That, to my way of thinking, is perfection." He kissed her again. "I wager, Miss Atwood, that we shall have a very happy future together."

She would have added her voice in agreement if he had allowed it, for she could not imagine a future that would be more wonderful than one with him. However, he did not allow her to utter even one word in agreement since he had once again claimed her mouth for a passionate kiss.

Instead, her contented, sigh of pleasure would have to suffice.

Behind them, Pythias snorted and stamped. Across the aisle, Hugo answered in kind. Outside the stables, grooms went about their duties, and not one of those things intruded upon Robert and Addie's thoughts. All these things were but a beautiful backdrop to a promising future – one, which would be filled with love and adventure, and on which, with an unusual upbringing for a daughter he loved more fiercely than she could ever love a horse, a father had wagered and won.

Before You Go

If you enjoyed this book, be sure to let others know by leaving a review.

~*~*~

Want to know when the next book in this series will be available?

You can always know what's new with my books by subscribing to my mailing list.

(There will, of course, be a thank you gift for joining because I think my readers are awesome!)

Book News from Leenie Brown

(bit.ly/LeenieBBookNews)

~*~*~

Turn the page to read an excerpt of another one of Leenie's books

His Beautiful Bea Excerpt

[If you enjoy books based on *Mansfield Park*, then you might like *His Beautiful Bea*, an original sweet Regency romance, written with intentional nods to *Mansfield Park*, and the first book in my *Touches of Austen Collection*. In this book, Graeme Clayton attempts to help his neighbour Beatrice Tierney capture the heart of his younger brother, but things don't quite go according to plan.]

CHAPTER 1

Beatrice Tierney blew out a breath and settled back against a tree in Stratsbury Park's garden, attempting to find a comfortable position in which to read. The weather was warm, but not unbearably so, and the shade cast by the sprawling canopy overhead provided a pleasant respite from the rays of the sun. A breeze occasionally fluttered the hem of her skirt and attempted to turn the pages of her book. All in all, it would be a perfect summer day, were it not for her cousins, Felicity and Grace Love. Bea's lips twitched with displeasure as she turned her attention back to the page she had read twice already.

She brushed away a fly that was meandering a path across the words she was attempting to decipher just as a long shadow crossed the page, causing her to look up to see its source.

"Is it a difficult passage?" Graeme Clayton stood looking down at her. He chuckled as her lips puckered into a deeper scowl. He knew very well that Bea was not short on intelligence. She might be quiet and verging on the edge of overly reserved and gentle, but it was not due to lack of intellect. In fact, when she did open her mouth and speak on any subject, her comments were often impressively well-thought-out. He knew that she studied things — mulling them over and over, assessing them from every possible angle, and then, and only then, having decided she had a good grasp of her ideas, her thoughts on a matter might be shared. Equally as often as not, however, she would merely smile softly, raise a brow, and remain silent. It perplexed him how she could keep her opinions to herself so often. He had a devil of a time keeping his tongue from saying exactly what was in his head.

Today, for the past twenty minutes, he had been observing her as she attempted to read and not watch his younger brother, Everett, and her cousin Felicity. She had sighed and shaken her head often, her lips had pursed, her brows had furrowed, and the pages of her book had not flipped in all that time. She was contemplating something, and he was rather certain he knew what it was.

Bea had always followed his brother around with a particular look on her face that spoke of her adoration of him. It was not an obvious expression. It was a particular softness in her eyes and the tipping up ever so slightly of the corners of her mouth.

He took a seat next to her on the ground and, giving her shoulder a nudge with his, repeated his question, earning him a very pretty scowl. However, as quickly as the scowl had formed on her lips, it melted away into the pleasant expression she wore in company when she would rather be elsewhere but did not wish to offend.

She was about to deny there was any issue at all — much as she always did. Others were permitted to be displeased and out of sorts, but Bea never allowed herself to be so — at least, not in company. One had to look for more subtle clues as to how Bea was really feeling, but that was just one thing what made her uniquely his Bea.

"No," she began her denial, just as he had predicted in his mind that she would, "the passage is not difficult. I was just distracted by the excellence of the weather."

Graeme, who was not content to let the situation pass so neatly, snatched her book out of her hands. It might be entirely possible to provoke her into revealing the truth of what he suspected. "Your distraction has nothing to do with my brother?" he asked as he snapped the book closed on her marker. Ah, there was her look of panic — a slight widening of the eyes and a sharp, though quiet, inhale of breath. He had obviously hit on the very thing which she was valiantly attempting to conceal.

Though they were only neighbours, Bea and her brother, Maxwell, had spent so many hours in company with Graeme and Everett that Graeme felt he knew the Tierney siblings almost as well as he knew his own brother. Well, "only neighbours" was perhaps not the most accurate way to describe who the Tierneys were to the Claytons.

Captain Tierney and Sir William Clayton had been friends since childhood, and when the captain had come into some money — enough to buy a small estate for his family — he had settled on Heathcote which was not more than four miles distance from the west of Stratsbury Park. And in such a manner had begun a closer friendship between their families. They spent many a day and evening in one another's company during that first month after the Tierneys' arrival at Heathcote.

And then had come the day when Captain Tierney had been required to return to his ship. He had called on his friend Sir Herbert the evening before and extracted a promise to care for Mrs. Tierney and his children if something unfortunate should befall him. As fate would have it, the unfortunate did befall the captain, and he had never returned from sea.

Bea had borne the news with far more fortitude than Graeme had expected to find in one so young and female. It was then that he had taken a greater liking to her. She was not like the silly girls he had met over the years. She was unique in her quiet strength and resolve. And so very unlike himself that he found himself compelled to attempt an understanding of such a person. His reward had been a comfortable friendship that allowed him access to the Beatrice others looking on would likely not suspect existed.

He nudged her shoulder again. "I do not believe it was the weather disturbing your reading," he whispered. "Are you positive your distraction has nothing to do with my brother?"

Bea shrugged.

Seeing he was not likely to get more of a reply from Bea than that, Graeme switched tactics and pressed on. "Miss Love is very pretty. How old is she now?"

Bea heaved a sigh. "Felicity is nineteen, just as I am, and Grace is seventeen."

"Are they both out?" he asked, moving her book away from the hand that attempted to reclaim it. He was not leaving this spot today without finding out if his suspicions about Bea's feelings for his brother were correct.

"Yes," Bea's lips stretched into a thin smile. "I have been regaled with the delights of the season several times since their arrival a fortnight ago."

Graeme shifted, placing the book on the grass next to him and stretching out his legs.

"Will you be going to town this next season? I could make a good number of introductions for you, and even with your modest dowry, I believe, we could find you a suitable husband."

He had not even finished speaking before her head was shaking back and forth.

"You will not go? I thought Max said he had put aside enough to give you a bit of a season."

"I do not wish to go. I have no desire to endure the crushes about which my cousins have told me. I prefer our small assemblies here."

"I imagine it will be harder to find a gentleman worthy of you here, but I have not been to an assembly in some time. Perhaps there is someone who has already captured your heart?" He tipped his head and studied her face carefully, looking for any indication that there might be a gentleman she already preferred.

The signs he sought were there — the slight blush on her cheek and the lowering of her eyes — but he chose to ignore them and continued on. "There is always Bath. I would assume the crowds are not so great as in London, and Mother has been forever begging father to take her there. I am certain she would enjoy taking you along. She does enjoy your company."

Bea ran a finger absent-mindedly along the chain that

held a pendant Graeme knew contained a lock of her father's hair. Between that action and the way she had pulled the corner of her bottom lip between her teeth, he knew she was considering the possibility of going to Bath. However, as fascinating as that fact was, it did not help him discern her feelings about his brother. So, he circled around to Everett once again. "Everett is planning one last go of the season before he takes up his position."

Bea nodded. "I know."

There was an interesting sadness to her tone. "Unless, of course, he finds a lady before then. Perhaps Miss Love will be capable of finally snaring him."

There it was — a small, sad, fleeting frown. It was true. Beatrice Tierney was in love with his brother — the fortunate clod. Hailed as the more studious of the two Clayton brothers, what Everett possessed in the ability to apply himself to his studies and excel, he lacked in his capacity to see the subtly obvious before him. However, Graeme would contemplate how his brother could have missed recognizing Bea's preference for him later. Right now, he needed to make Bea smile.

"Many have tried to bring him up to snuff, you know, but none have succeeded. He is a handsome devil — much like his older brother."

Bea chuckled. "He is, at least, more humble than his brother," she chided.

"So, you do not deny that the Clayton brothers are handsome?" Graeme teased.

Bea rolled her eyes. "I am not blind," she said with a light swat to Graeme's arm.

"Neither am I," Graeme retorted.

Bea's brows furrowed in confusion.

"I am not speaking of being blind to my own comeliness," he smiled at her. "For I assure you that I know precisely how fetching I look." He winked and then chuckled as she once again rolled her eyes. It was always a joy to provoke her just enough to elicit a small response such as he had just received.

"I see many things clearly. For instance, I can see that Miss Love and Miss Grace are attractive and well-skilled in all the arts required to capture a husband." He shrugged. "There are many such ladies in London, who, if they wish a desired outcome, will do their best to achieve it no matter the ploys and scheming necessary."

He nodded in response to her wide-eyed questioning look. "A fellow has to tread carefully. However, that is not all I see clearly."

"It is not?"

"No, it is not." He crossed his arms and leaned against the trunk of the tree, his shoulder brushing against hers, and his arm wishing to wrap around her and pull her close to his side as he had done when she was just a girl. However, she was no longer a mere child, and he was not her brother, so unless he wished to get scolded and have her dash away, neither of which would assist his cause, he refrained.

"I also see the way you look at my brother, and frankly, he is a fool to ignore you. I would not ignore a lady of beauty and good character such as yourself if she was to look at me so longingly." He pressed his lips together to keep from chuckling at the quick breath she drew. He had shocked her just as he had planned.

"I do no such thing," Bea refuted weakly.

"Lying does not become you, my beautiful Bea."

"Do not call me that. I am not beautiful."

He peeked over at her. Her cheeks were aflame as he knew they would be. "My dear, if there is one thing I know, it is beautiful women, and you are definitely beautiful – beguiling, even, when you blush so prettily." He reached out a hand and grabbed her arm to prevent her from jumping to her feet and running away. Bea did not like compliments of her person or actions. She preferred to fade into the background — to act without recognition or praise, qualities that would serve a parson's wife well, but also qualities that made it easy for a numbskull, soon-to-be parson, like his brother to overlook her.

"Now," he said, holding her arm firmly as she tried to pull it out of his grasp, "as I have said, I am of the belief that my brother is an idiot and Miss Love is a grasping...," he cleared his throat, "something that is not appropriate for a lady's ears."

Bea's eyes grew wide, and her head tilted as she looked out toward where Felicity was talking in a very animated fashion to her sister while clinging to Everett's arm.

"I saw both her and her sister in London," Graeme whispered near Bea's ear.

"Then, why did you ask me if they were both out?" She gasped as his lips brushed her cheek when she turned her head.

He smirked and shrugged. "I am a cad and wished to hear your opinion of them."

"Which I did not give," she pulled on her arm again, finally freeing it from his hold.

"Oh, but you did," he replied. "Your tone and the shortness of your replies told me all I need to know. You are not pleased with them — or more precisely, you are not pleased with Miss Love since she is the one who has enchanted my brother."

"I have never enjoyed my cousins," she refuted. "We have little in common. They like fashion and soirees while I prefer books and domestic pursuits. However, you have never been home when they visited before so you would not know how very unalike we are."

He chuckled. "Deny it if you must, but you are jealous." He climbed to his feet and extended a hand to her.

Bea looked at his hand warily.

"Come, you cannot sit here the full day. Mother will wish to know you took some exercise. She worries about you."

Bea's brows furrowed as she studied his face. "You will not say shocking things, and your lips will not touch me?"

A hint of mischief touched his smile. "You know I am constitutionally incapable of not saying something shocking at some point, but I shall refrain from touching any part of you other than your fingers with my lips."

Bea sighed and shook her head, but a touch of amusement curled her lips into a small smile as she placed her hand in his and allowed him to help her to her feet.

"Good heavens," he muttered as he pulled her upright, "if my brother does not marry you, I might. When you smile like that, it is difficult not to wish to break my promise to confine my lips to just your fingers."

He winked as her mouth dropped open. "As I said, I am constitutionally incapable of not being shocking." He tucked her hand into the crook of his arm.

He was teasing her, of course — at least, partially. She was both beautiful and beguiling, and were she not so obviously lovesick for his brother and were she not Bea, his friend and the closest thing he had to a sister, he would be hard-pressed not to consider her as the next Lady Clayton.

Continue reading *His Beautiful Bea*

Acknowledgements

There are many who have had a part in the creation of this story. Some have read and commented on it. Some have proofread for grammatical errors and plot holes. Others have not even read the story and a few, I know, will never read it. However, their encouragement and belief in my ability, as well as their patience when I became cranky or when supper was late or the groceries ran low, was invaluable.

And so, I would like to say *thank you* to Zoe, Rose, Kristine, Ben, and Kyle. I feel blessed through your help, support, and understanding.

I have not listed my dear husband in the above group because, to me, he deserves his own special thank you, for, without his somewhat pushy insistence that I start sharing my writing, none of my writing goals and dreams would have been met.

~*~*~

For those who might be interested, I have some visual inspiration, as well as a couple of research sources, pinned to a board on Pinterest. You can find that board at this link: bit.ly/Pinterest_Addie.

Other Leenie B Books

You can find all of Leenie's books at this link
bit.ly/LeenieBBooks
where you can explore the collections below

~*~

Other Pens, Mansfield Park

~*~

Touches of Austen Collection

~*~

Dash of Darcy and Companions Collection

~*~

Marrying Elizabeth Series

~*~

Willow Hall Romances

~*~

The Choices Series

~*~

Darcy Family Holidays

~*~

Darcy and... An Austen-Inspired Collection

About the Author

Leenie Brown has always been a girl with an active imagination, which, while growing up, was both an asset, providing many hours of fun as she played out stories, and a liability, when her older sister and aunt would tell her frightening tales. At one time, they had her convinced Dracula lived in the trunk at the end of the bed she slept in when visiting her grandparents!

Although it has been years since she cowered in her bed in her grandparents' basement, she still has an imagination which occasionally runs away with her, and she feeds it now as she did then — by reading!

Her heroes, when growing up, were authors, and the worlds they painted with words were (and still are) her favourite playgrounds! Now, as an adult, she spends much of her time in the Regency world, playing with the characters from her favourite Jane Austen novels and those of her own creation.

When she is not traipsing down a trail in an attempt to keep up with her imagination, Leenie resides in the beautiful province of Nova Scotia with her two sons and her very own Mr. Brown (a wonderful mix of all the best of Darcy, Bingley, and Edmund with a healthy dose of the teasing Mr. Tilney and just a dash of the scolding Mr. Knightley).

Connect with Leenie

E-mail:

LeenieBrownAuthor@gmail.com

Facebook:

www.facebook.com/LeenieBrownAuthor

Blog:

leeniebrown.com

Patreon:

https://www.patreon.com/LeenieBrown

Subscribe to Leenie's Mailing List:

Book News from Leenie Brown

(bit.ly/LeenieBBookNews)

www.ingramcontent.com/pod-product-compliance
Lightning Source LLC
Chambersburg PA
CBHW022152240626
47153CB00007B/2621